APRIL O'CONNELL

I0743477

CURL UP AND DIE

Copyright © 2020 April O'Connell

This is a work of fiction.
Names, characters, businesses, places, events, locales, and incidents are either the products of the author's imagination or used in a fictitious manner. Any resemblance to actual persons, living or dead, or actual events is purely coincidental.

All rights reserved. No portion of this book may be reproduced, scanned, or distributed in any printed or electronic form without permission. Please do not participate in or encourage piracy of copyrighted materials in violation of the author's rights.

Purchase only authorized editions.

ISBN: 978-1-945169-37-3

Orison Publishers, Inc.
PO Box 188
Grantham, PA 17027
717-731-1405
www.OrisonPublishers.com
Publish your book now, marsha@orisonpublishers.com

Printed in the United States of America

This story is dedicated

to my mother,

who encourages me to keep going

and my daughter,

who fills my life with laughter and love.

CHAPTER ONE

Rachel stood on the steps outside her apartment building. She hesitantly looked at her watch to check the time.

"Crap, I'm going to be late again!"

Her nemesis has always been timeliness. Running late and practically running down the street as usual, she didn't care that she was going to catch hell for the hundredth time—not today.

Rachel Perry kept up the pace from her apartment on East Marion, to the salon located on Orange Street in Lancaster.

The city streets were lined with old colonial red brick buildings, art galleries, small specialty shops, and quaint little restaurants. Everything the city's inhabitants needed was within walking distance, so they moved with purpose like pedestrians from an even bigger city.

It was not surprising that no one paid any attention to the loud clatter made by Rachel's boots smacking against the pavement. She moved at an amazing speed for a woman in her favorite, black, high-heeled boots.

The wind froze her to the core. Not one to put practicality before fashion, Rachel never wore a down-lined jacket. She always thought they made people look fat. Especially the white ones. They gave the appearance of ginormous marshmallows stacked on top of one another. She wasn't about to let anything make her figure look like a marshmallow. Gloves were fine. Who cared if your hands looked fat?

As she tossed her red hair over her shoulder, the wind caught it and tousled and twisted it around her face, adding to her disheveled appearance—so much for looking put together.

Rachel was in no mood to start her workday with any crap from anyone. She walked with the edge of a woman scorned. Her favorite black boots pounded the pavement with every angry step she took. She was as mad as hell. Her reddened face matched her fiery hair that looked as though it could blaze at any moment. Rachel huffed as she turned the corner and stormed into the salon.

Shirley's Hair and Nail Salon was buzzing with patrons as usual. Women in all stages of beauty sat under dryers, read the latest trash magazines while waiting their turn or chatted loudly about who was cheating, who was pregnant, or any other dirt they heard throughout the week. Some locals stopped for the company, the gossip, and a cup of coffee. It looked more like a social event for middle aged women than a place of business. It was the place to learn all the newest gossip, to work out your marriage issues, or spew your drama to an active audience. There was no shortage of advice givers, rumor spreaders, or man-hating comments.

The salon had the distinct smell of perm solution, coffee, and a mixture of nail enhancement chemicals and hair spray. The locals loved it.

The bell on the door rang loudly and all heads turned to see who was joining their little party. Rachel slammed the door a little harder than she intended. Shirley's head shot up at the banging of her door and her scowl could be viewed in every available mirror in the salon.

Rachel avoided eye contact with Shirley and everyone else who was staring at her as she continued her journey. Her abrupt mumbled hello to everyone was enough to give away her pissed off mood as was the angry look on her face that made her green eyes glow with fury.

Her fast-paced movements and the loud clicking of her footsteps against the wooden floors made the clients and her co-workers exchange knowing glances. Gossip was about to ensue. Rachel's mood and what or who had caused it was already buzzing around the room like killer bees that had suddenly swarmed the place. No one doubted it was caused by a man. All other topics were off the table as the women tried to determine the particulars. There were lots of hushed whisperers that had their theories growing in the pass-it-down-the-lane structure that happened when women wanted all the juicy details of another woman's mystery and anger. They had the man pegged a bastard before they even knew his name. Other women had a knack of knowing when a woman's mood was directly related to the actions of the male species, and Rachel was a force to be reckoned with, they shared with one another.

Rachel's scowl had that *go-to-the-devil* look and that was exactly how she felt toward every man alive. Well, maybe just one man. She stomped into the back room, shook out of her white faux fur jacket, and closed the door with a bang that was louder than her boss, Shirley, would have liked.

The salon became silent as the stylists and clients exchanged glances again.

Because it was so out of character for Rachel to exhibit such a display of anger, her best friend and co-worker, Valerie Meadows, couldn't wait to finish up with her hot-blooded and out of place male client's haircut. She needed to find out all about Rachel's reason for her pissed off mood. There was no doubt in Valerie's mind that Rachel's mood was directly related to the date Rachel had the night before. She warned her not to go, but Rachel was worn down by the persistence of that hot-looking man. She was only human, after all. At some point, a girl just had to go for it. From the looks of things, Rachel went for it and it turned out just as painful as a root canal.

Valerie loved juicy details, the bitter disappointments, the happiness and the tears, and the glorious conversations about sex lives. The more drama from others the less thought she gave to her own messed up life. Focusing on her best friend for the day would be a great distraction.

The two women shared every detail of their lives. Valerie was already aware of Rachel's apprehensions of dating the Dickster, as they nicknamed Richard Reynolds. The excitement of good gossip filled Valerie, who was bursting at the seams of her black spandex pants.

Valerie exchanged glances with the salon owner, Shirley, who only looked back at the slammed door, let out a sigh, and rolled her eyes. Shirley did take a second to look at the clock and made a mental note of Rachel's habitual tardiness. She gave up lecturing both girls on the importance of being on time. Why waste her breath? Instead, when the time was right, Shirley would get in a few digs. Maybe someday it would sink in. She could always give Rachel some extra laundry duties for her serious lack of time awareness. Rachel hated folding towels with a passion. Shirley smiled to herself but decided to let Rachel cool off before she would punish her. That is what a good boss would do, Shirley told herself.

Valerie finished with her client and rushed to the back room. Her four inch red heels did not seem to slow her down as they clinked against the polished wooden floor. She opened the door and stood in the doorway. Tapping her foot and leaning on the doorframe, Valerie watched Rachel sitting at the two-seater lunch table rummaging through her over-sized, leopard-print, faux designer handbag. Rachel was pulling items out of the purse and throwing them haphazardly on top of the table. The pile was starting to take on a life of its own.

Valerie took inventory of the growing mountain of used tissues, her own favorite missing lip-gloss that she planned to steal back from Rachel, a compact, vent brush, balled-up miscellaneous receipts, Rachel's matching leopard-print wallet and her pink-cased iPhone. The scene made Valerie smile as she pondered why women felt the need to carry so much shit around with them. It was no wonder they were always complaining about back and shoulder pain. All that stuff added up. She decided to try gently approaching her friend.

"You, uh, looking for a screwdriver in that mess?" Valerie teased. "And I'd like my lip-gloss back, please. You knew I was searching for that and all this time you had it, you thief," Valerie teased.

"Dumb bastard. He's such a prick," Rachel murmured under her breath.

She began pulling out her small, black leather bag containing her favorite pair of cutting shears. She grabbed the lip-gloss and tossed it to Valerie, who successfully caught the colorful missile with one hand and tossed her long black hair with the other.

"Hey, you alright?" Valerie frowned as she cautiously approached Rachel.

"Oh, I'll live," Rachel murmured as she sank a little lower into the seat. She leaned forward, resting her head in her hands and crushing the handbag on her lap. Her face seemed swallowed up by a sea of massive, red hair that fell around her small, slightly freckled face. Her expression changed from pissed off to woe-is-me in a heartbeat.

Valerie entered the room farther and knelt beside her friend. She grabbed both of Rachel's hands and brought her friend around to face her. She did not like the look in Rachel's reddened green eyes. Her flaming hair seemed even redder against the flushed look of her normally white cheeks.

"Rach, what's wrong?" Valerie questioned with the calmest voice that she could muster.

"Nothing," Rachel answered, releasing her hands and giving her handbag a toss onto the nearby chair. She missed her target and the rest of the handbag's contents spilled all over the floor.

"Damn it all to hell!" Rachel shrieked as she pulled farther away from Valerie and flopped onto the floor to pick up her belongings. She frantically looked for her favorite mega mascara that had rolled under a utility cart. Rachel rammed the cart away and scooped up her mascara, only to throw it back into her handbag.

Valerie knew Rachel Perry well enough to know her exasperating behavior would be short lived. Rachel usually did not carry on like a crazy person. She was usually the voice of reason. Because time was ticking and Valerie was dying for information, she decided to get to the point and poke the angry bear.

"Come on, Rachel. Don't make me pull it out of your ass today," Valerie said, applying a healthy layer of her newly re-acquired lip gloss to her full lips. "I had to deal with Mrs. Groff this morning and she was twenty minutes early, waiting at the door for me to show up. You know how obnoxious and mean-spirited her comments are. It's always the same blah, blah, blah bullshit. Don't brush so hard, you're parting it the wrong way, you cut it too short, the cape is too tight. Wa,wa,wa!"

Rachel had to smile at Valerie's perfect imitation of Mrs. Groff's nasally voice.

Valerie, seeing the smile, continued with the morning's events.

"I made the cape overly tight on purpose. I wanted to strangle the old hag and put her out of my misery. Seriously, I am starting to fight a severe headache. What is it? Your date with Richard go bad last night or is it something else?"

"Don't say that bastard's name. He is the most arrogant, unfeeling asshole that I've ever met!" Rachel balled up another tissue and threw it, missing the trash can by several inches. She stuck up her finger at it and left the tissue right where it landed.

Valerie walked over to put the tissue in the trash can. Her headache was increasing by the second.

"Come on, Rachel, seriously? Spit it out!" Valerie's patience waned. She was starting to lose her temper.

Angry tears stung Rachel's eyes as she looked up at her friend and most trusted confidant. Rachel sighed and decided to answer Valerie's inquisition.

"Remember when I said I was breaking my rule about going out with any man named Richard? That they're always dicks? Well, he didn't disappoint."

"That bastard! I did warn you, Rach," Valerie said smugly.

"I am so pissed off! I actually fell for it and slept with him!" Rachel's shrilled response drilled into Valerie's throbbing head. Valerie rubbed at her temples, closed her eyes, and let out a huge sigh.

"Right, well, common sense would say, when you date someone nick-named the Dickster, he's got one thing on his mind and it ain't wining and dining; it's gettin' lucky. Again, I told you not to go, remember?"

"I know, I know. Nevertheless, he is amazingly handsome and his body was, uh…" Rachel paused.

Valerie smiled at Rachel's inability to talk about his maleness out loud. "So, what I am gathering is his nickname implies more than just his arrogant personality. He's put together nicely in that area."

Rachel blushed. "I don't remember."

"Liar," Valerie smiled.

"He all but begged me with those big, amazing doe-eyes and I melted. Plus, I haven't had a steady boyfriend in a while and I was getting a little…"

Valerie started to laugh. "A little what? Hungry for the sausage sandwich? Famished for bumping uglies? It's okay to want sex, Rachel. You know people have been doing it since the beginning of time. And you don't need to have a steady boyfriend to have sex."

"Yeah, well I'm a little more selective with whom I choose to sleep."

"Ouch! I'm hurt. Oh, I thought of another one. Having someone stir your paint."

Rachel had to laugh at the last slang that Valerie came up with for her benefit.

"I guess it has been a long time since someone dipped their paint brush."

"It's stir your paint, but I like that one!" It has been too long for you, which is why you got all horny and ended up spending the night with the Dickster. If you would have been *feeding the need* more often, maybe he would not have looked so appealing and maybe you would not be so upset today. Ever think of that?"

"Nobody thinks of that. Only you would think of that."

"That's because I'm smart and the most amazing friend on the planet."

"Humble. You forgot humble, Val."

"Yeah and humble and sexy and..."

"Alright, alright, I get it. You are awesome, now let me sulk a little more and I'll be ready to go."

Valerie moved to the door and tossed her hair over her shoulder as she sent a huge smile to her friend.

"So, we'll talk more about your man issue later. Gather yourself together because your first one is Dolores Harrison. She looks about as upset as you do today. Maybe that ass-brained husband of hers finally was caught or one of his whores gave him something more than a good time, if you know what I mean. Come on out in a few minutes; I'll stall for you," Valerie said. She left the room shaking her head and rubbing at her temples.

Rachel poured herself a cup of coffee and took a few deep, cleansing breaths. Meditation skills were surely what she needed. How did others deal with anxiety and disappointment? Alcohol came to mind and she decided that it would help more to visit a bar than try to meditate the Dickster out of her mind. As she took her first sip, the steaming java burnt her lip and that sent her into another swearing fit. She yelled skyward, blaming God for her string of bad luck. She knew through her Christian upbringing that God was not to blame for her stream of near misses and bad breaks. Rachel grabbed a used tissue from the top of the mound of handbag clutter and dabbed at her burnt lip. She made a mental note to say a prayer and ask God for his forgiveness. Rachel thought she would throw in a few more self-serving requests while she was at it. A mischievous smirk crossed her face when she thought to add a lightning bolt to hit Richard and fry his paint brush clean off.

She scooped up the pile of mess and threw the contents back into her purse. Rachel knew that she had wasted enough time and hated making any of her clients wait too long. She took a deep breath, let it out slowly and pulled herself together before she left the back room.

As she entered the cutting area, Rachel could feel that all eyes were on her and a hush fell over the room. Her attempts at a smile felt like torture, but she put one on her face and tried to look and sound as professional as possible.

Shirley let out a grunting sound but never made eye contact with Rachel. It was her way of letting her employee know that there would be hell to pay if Rachel did not get herself moving.

Rachel placed her coffee and her shears on the top of her work cart. As she turned toward the mirror, she got a good look at Dolores Harrison's reflection. Valerie's observation was dead on. Dolores looked like she was ready to explode. Her hands were clamped tightly around a tissue and a deep frown was making her look older than her 50-plus years. She was definitely not in a good mood. Rachel would bet her next paycheck that Dolores was also suffering from man issues. She had seen Dolores look the same way in the past. It always stemmed from her husband, Mayor Oliver Harrison.

"He needs a bullet to his head, the cheating bastard," Rachel mumbled under her breath.

The two women had a long history together. Rachel met Dolores when she dated Dolores' son, Nick. During Rachel's few semesters spent at Penn State, she fell hopelessly in love with Nick Harrison and he with her. Rachel and Nick became so inseparable that they spent every waking moment that they could spare in each other's company. They even split holidays and vacations with their families so that they did not have to be apart. Rachel's attorney father and her stay-at-home mother did not like sharing their only child with another family during the holidays. That is, of course, unless it meant that Rachel was marrying into the kind of money that the Harrisons clearly possessed.

When Nick's well-to-do parents invited Rachel to visit any time she wished, well, at least Dolores wanted her around, Rachel spent time on holidays at their home. She would help Dolores decorate, cook the meals and bake. She became a second mother to Rachel. She did not share the same warm feelings with Oliver that she did with Dolores. Upon meeting Oliver, Rachel immediately felt belittled by his disapproving gazes. She took a fast dislike for the man who spent more time looking at her ass than her face. After Rachel dropped out of college and entered cosmetology school, her relationship with Nick fizzled. Because Oliver Harrison decided that Rachel was a quitter, unsuitable for his son, and would hold his son back. He said as much to her face over their Thanksgiving dinner. Nick never wanted to displease his successful father. He not only didn't stand up for her, he broke her heart and dumped her before the leftover Thanksgiving turkey hit the fridge. Rachel concluded that the man who held the money held the power.

Dolores was depressed at the thought of losing the girl that she hoped would become her daughter-in-law. Dolores could afford to go anywhere for her hair and nail appointments, but she decided that the way to keep Rachel in her life was to become her client. She started visiting the cosmetology school in Lancaster that Rachel attended. When the students had days to work in the school's salon, Dolores would let her practice on her hair color, haircut, and nails. Some visits were more successful than others. However, Dolores liked the passion and happiness she saw in Rachel's face when she finally caught on to the proper way to hold her shears and the angles it took to get the desired result, or when she formulated the color perfectly. The nails were another story. Acrylic nails took Rachel longer to figure out. She never gave up and eventually worked with the acrylic perfectly.

Over the past seven years, she followed Rachel to two different salons and watched Rachel's skills blossom. Dolores secretly wished her wishy-washy son would reconnect with Rachel, giving her the daughter that she desperately wanted.

Dolores attempted a smile as she saw Rachel's gaze in the mirror.

"I'm ready for you, Dolores. Come on over," Rachel said, as she wiped stray hairs from her chair. "Can I take your coat?"

Dolores hugged Rachel, swung out of her coat and into the empty chair. Rachel mechanically hung up the coat, placed the cape around Dolores' neck, and began to pump up the chair. Rachel tried not to think about her man issues as she began to comb out Dolores' level seven, brown ash-colored hair.

Dolores had worn her hair in the same style for all of the years that Rachel had known her. She never changed her conservative, short, curled style. The boring color had been the same for seven years. How Rachel had wanted and encouraged Dolores to change it up. Sadly, she was never able to convince her to try something new.

Rachel practically fell backward when Dolores decided to address her boring, stately, hairstyle and color.

"Rachel, what do you think about coloring and highlighting my hair? I was also thinking about changing the cut. Maybe we could update my look or something."

Dolores felt as other women did, that if she changed her hair, it could somehow fix her problems. She assumed many women looked to change their outward appearance as a fix for what was wrong on the inside. She studied herself in the mirror and frowned.

Rachel dropped her comb and stared at Dolores' in the mirror. There was a swirl of emotions in her tired brown eye. The lines on her face seemed deeper. Her energy was depression and anxiety that whirled around her. Rachel bent down to pick up her comb and placed it in her sanitation jar. She opened up her station drawer and pulled out a clean comb. She couldn't think of how to answer Dolores.

Dolores's hands went up to her hair. She tried to adjust her bangs to cover more of her forehead. She slid her fingers down to rest on both sides of her face and pulled her skin back. It was a feeble attempt to look younger. Dolores used all of the expensive wrinkle-reducing, age-defying products she could get her hands on.

"Maybe I should have you dye this hair. Dye it a darker brown, like when I was younger. I used to have the most beautiful chestnut-brown hair when I was a child. Maybe you could put some pretty highlights in it. Subtle, nothing too dramatic, just something to make me look younger," Dolores looked pleadingly at Rachel's reflection.

Rachel absentmindedly began to comb Dolores' hair. A stress headache began to slowly work its way from her shoulders, her neck and traveled to her forehead.

"You dye Easter eggs, but you color hair," Rachel thoughtlessly stated. Suddenly aware of her harsh tone, Rachel blushed and met Dolores' somber stare. "I'm sorry, Dolores. That was rude of me. It's a hair stylist's pet peeve. The word dye.

Rachel wasn't making any sense to Dolores. She failed to see the difference between dyeing hair and coloring it; they meant the same to her.

Rachel could see the confused look on Dolores' face.

"I'm not feeling like myself today," Rachel stated with a guilt-ridden expression on her face. "Let's start small with the changes." Rachel forced a smile. "We can always do more if you like it. What about starting with a new cut?" Rachel tried to sound more cheerful.

Dolores smiled slightly. "That sounds good. If I like it, maybe next week we can color it, alright?"

"Yes, I will book more time in my schedule, just in case you want to do it. See, great minds think alike, Dolores," Rachel answered as she continued combing through the massive amount of hair-sprayed helmet hair.

Dolores could not help but wonder why Rachel stormed into the salon earlier. Rachel rarely showed her temperament in that way. She was always friendly and upbeat. Dolores decided to cautiously approach the subject. She needed a distraction from her own miserable life.

"Rachel, are you alright?" Dolores carefully whispered.

Rachel looked around the room and noticed that several of the Gossip Gals Gang, as she liked to call them, purposely tried to eavesdrop on their conversation.

"Oh, let's just say last night was a disaster."

"Really, how so?" Dolores' soft brown eyes looked intently at Rachel in the mirror.

"You know how men can be. They have a one-track mind. From the very beginning, they say the right things, practically beg you to have dinner, some buy you flowers, some chocolate. It's all in an attempt to hook up. They throw the "L" word in for good measure if they think it will lead to dipping their paint brush in your paint."

Dolores gasped and Valerie laughed loudly when she heard Rachel tell Dolores about the brush and the paint. Valerie decided to crush all attempts to satisfy the chatter of the Gossip Gals Gang. She spoke loudly over the sound of her dryer.

"Rachel, I am so glad you are feeling better. Cramps are no way to start your day. No wonder you were so pissed earlier. Heavy flow days are no joke."

As quick as a bald man's haircut, the gang turned back to Shirley's new complaint about her husband, Carl. Other women never liked to hear complaints about the monthly flow. *Suffer in silence* was the unspoken mantra of any women that still suffered the monthly interruption.

Dolores took the opportunity to speak freely with Rachel. It was a small town and the word got around that Rachel had a date with the Dickster.

"I take it your date with that Richard Reynolds fellow did not go so well. He tried dating you for months, as I recall. He was a real persistent bugger."

"Yeah, well I was right to hesitate. I have only myself to blame for getting a little tipsy at a party we went to. The party was thrown by some mutual acquaintances. That's why I agreed to go. I had way too much to drink. Not fruity wine either. I was drinking apple whiskey mixed with soda and on an empty stomach.

"Rachel, that's not good. You should have eaten something."

"Well, the party throwers are vegans and they insisted on serving soy meat that resembled turkey, a larger-than-life salad, corn chips, a vegan dip for vegetables and other stuff that just wasn't my vibe. Not that I don't appreciate their life choices, I do. I just don't want to be one. And I wouldn't throw a party and expect them to eat meat. Had there been steaks for the meat lovers, or even hotdogs that were made from questionable meat, I would have dived in."

"That doesn't sound like much fun."

"Oh, I had a great time. But carrot sticks dipped in non-dairy ranch didn't cut it for me. I let the Dickster come back to my place and I slept with him."

"Didn't your roommate mind?"

"Angela left to spend the night at her mother's house. Her mother just got out of the hospital from her hysterectomy, so Angela wanted to be with her for her first night home."

"That was very thoughtful of her. I really like your roommate. Angie seems to be clean and tidy. She dresses smartly and keeps to herself."

"Yeah, she's a gem, "Rachel said with sarcasm in her voice. Not wanting to discuss Angela's attributes, she decided to change the subject.

"So, anyway, I woke up alone. He just grabbed his stuff and left without a single word to me. I feel foolish and used. It was really a bad, bad choice on my part."

"Oh my, Rachel, I hope you were safe. That is, I hope you...uh, used… a condom. Protection," Dolores whispered and turned several shades of red.

"Yeah that's the one thing I seem to do right when it comes to men. He did not wake me, just got his shit, I mean stuff and he left. It made me feel like some cheap whore or something. If I ever see him again, I'll take a baseball bat to his balls."

"Batter up!" Valerie added with a laugh. "Get it, Rach? Up?"

Dolores couldn't help but scowl.

Rachel saw Dolores become uncomfortable. She immediately regretted her tirade.

"I'm so sorry, Dolores. I shouldn't be talking like this in front of you." Rachel's cheeks flushed with embarrassment.

Dolores reached up and patted Rachel's hand. "Oh, nonsense, I am not offended. You don't have to guard yourself with me," she lied with a slight smile. She did not want Rachel to feel embarrassed. "There have been times when I wished I had a bat myself." Dolores was cringing on the inside. She could not help but wonder if Rachel's foul mouth was the direct result of her friendship with that trampy-looking Valerie Meadows girl. Dolores did not remember ever hearing Rachel have such a potty mouth before her friendship with Valerie. The woman oozed sexuality. Did she ever own a shirt that wasn't too small? Her shirts never seemed to cover her too-perky breasts. The cleavage she showed was sinful. Not to mention the spandex pants she wore with those high heels. Dolores thought Valerie was a prostitute because of the way she flirted with any man who dared to enter the salon.

Rachel led Dolores to the washbowl. Dolores leaned back in the bowl and adjusted herself. The water was a few degrees from scalding but didn't want to complain. She hoped Rachel would figure it out on her own.

Rachel applied the shampoo that Dolores liked. She scrubbed with more vigor than usual and Dolores decided it was best to try to calm Rachel down before she rubbed her thinning hair clean off her head.

"Rachel, I've known you for many years. I have confided more than my share of secrets."

"We both share."

"Remember what you always tell me?" Dolores asked.

"Yes, it's the hairstylist's motto—what it said in the salon stays in the salon."

"Do you mean it?"

"Do I mean what?" Rachel answered distractedly.

"Do you mean that I can tell you anything and it goes no further than the two of us?"

Rachel stopped scrubbing and looked down at Dolores with a curious look on her face.

"Dolores, you could tell me anything, I wouldn't tell a soul."

Dolores looked away briefly and let out a cleansing sigh. She closed her eyes for a moment.

Rachel looked around for eavesdroppers. Some of the Gossip Gal Gang had started to clear out. She saw Shirley was deep in conversation and perm rods, and Valerie was busy flirting with a new male client that had just come in. Valerie was the master of making men stupid with lust for her. She knew just how to use that curvy body and those big breasts to entice a man. Deciding that the coast was clear, Rachel gave her undivided attention to Dolores. "What is it? What's on your mind?" she questioned.

"I caught him again. I caught Oliver cheating on me. This time it is with his secretary. Excuse me, his administrative assistant,

Carla Cassidy. The stupid jerk has receipts in his sock drawer. His sock drawer!"

Tears rolled down Dolores' cheeks. She dabbed at her eyes with a tissue. Her bottom lip quivered. "He put them there knowing full well that I would find them. He is taunting me with her, throwing it right out in front of me to trip over. Well, the only thing I'm going to be tripping over is his dead body!" Dolores shook with anger. Her raised voice was loud enough to get the attention of the entire salon. Aware that her outburst was sure to draw attention, Dolores contracted into the chair and she grew silent as a few new tears ran from her eyes.

Rachel began a conditioning treatment and spoke in a whispered tone. "Do you honestly think he's that stupid? He cannot handle another scandal. It wasn't too long ago that the feds were investigating him for some shady investments, not to mention the affair with that woman reporter. He can't honestly think that being a mayor gives him power to be corrupt."

"Rachel, no one else knows about the government investigation. After the affair with the reporter, nothing she said was credible. It made her look like a bitter woman who got dumped. Oliver made sure to dig up dirt on her so that she lost all credibility. Trust me, I am probably not the only woman who wants my husband dead.

"You can add me to the list."

"The most frustrating part is he successfully kept his image squeaky clean enough to be running for the Senate."

"Are you serious, he's running for the Senate?" questioned Rachel.

"He plans to run this year, yes."

"I take it you are not a fan of being a Senator's wife?"

"No, I'm just not a fan of being Oliver's wife. Not anymore. I gave him thirty-five years of my life and he repays me with naked pictures of his secretary tucked in his sock drawer."

"Pictures too, huh?" whispered Rachel.

Dolores silently nodded her head. More tears flowed and it broke Rachel's heart. She did not understand how anyone would ever hurt such a wonderful and amazing woman. Oliver did not deserve such a remarkable, dedicated wife.

The two women made their way back to Rachel's station in silence and remained silent until Dolores' haircut was finished. It was the first time Dolores smiled since entering the salon. Her new style was just the right change she needed.

Rachel and Dolores retreated to the manicure and pedicure area located in the far corner of the salon. They were alone and could speak more freely. Rachel was the first to break their abnormal silence.

"If you need a place to get away, my apartment isn't much, but you're welcome anytime. I know my roommate wouldn't mind. Angela really likes you."

"Rachel, you are always kind and I do treasure you. You have been like a daughter to me and frankly, I do not know what I would do without your shoulder to cry on. Your friendship means so much to me. Not to mention, you have some wonderful hair teasing skills," Dolores said, forcing a smile.

Rachel chuckled. "Thank you, Dolores. I meant it, you are always welcome."

Dolores removed her hand from the manicure table and reached into her sweater pocket. She removed a small black notebook. "I also found this. I went searching in his home office for more evidence that he was cheating on me and found this hidden under his desk drawer. Look at the Velcro tabs on it. He had it stuck to the bottom of his desk. He must not want anyone to find it if he's hiding it that way."

"I agree," answered Rachel. "But why were you looking under his desk?"

"Oh, when we were in college together, Oliver would hide his most important stuff this way so that his snooping roommates wouldn't poke around in his things."

"Pretty clever trick," Rachel said.

"Yeah, Oliver is that clever. Clever as a fox. I was wondering if you would do me a favor."

"Sure, anything."

"Hold on to this book for me, alright?"

Rachel looked down at the book and took it from Dolores. "Sure. Won't he know it's missing?" Rachel was not exactly sure why Dolores wanted her to keep the book, but she did not see any harm in holding on to it for a while.

"He might miss it, yes. I don't care. It serves him right. But he can't say anything to me about it or ask me where it is. That would be admitting it was there in the first place. I have a few tricks of my own, Rachel. Hang on to it until I can decide what to do with it. It might be important enough to destroy his career. That's why I want you to hold on to it. He will never think to ask if you have it," confirmed Dolores.

Rachel tossed the book in her manicure drawer without a second thought. She reminded herself that later, she would put the book in the bottom of her purse. She knew no one was daring enough to go searching in there.

Dolores picked a blood-red OPI nail polish. It was from their Vampire Collection and cleverly named Dracula's Daiquiri.

Both women relaxed enough to enjoy the rest of their weekly visit. Their moods lifted as they changed their conversation to their favorite reality show's season finale, Dolores' latest book club meeting and the new clothing store that opened on Queen Street.

Dolores hugged Rachel before she left. "Don't forget to hide the book," she whispered in Rachel's ear.

CHAPTER
TWO

olores left the salon and began to finish her errands before going back home to Harrisburg. She purposely moved her hair and nail appointments to every other Friday to go to a popular market in Lancaster. *Kill two birds with one stone*, she thought.

She loved the feel of Central Market in the city. The charm of the old brick building, the hustle and bustle of customers purchasing their fruits, vegetables, and homemade breads normally made her feel cheerful. However, that day was not a normal day. She was a little envious of a simpler life. A life where she could go home, cook dinner, watch a movie or the evening news with a loving spouse and fall happily asleep next to him. Was there such a thing? Dolores wondered if the *happily ever after* was truly only in fairy tales or if some people found that special someone and felt those butterflies in their stomach. She was feeling something in her stomach when she thought of her husband. It was not even close to being butterflies. It was more like acid burning a hole from her throat to her stomach. A sadness washed over her as a tear slid down her cheek.

Betrayal was an evil thing. It made you doubt your life, your choices, yourself.

Her existence had always revolved around her husband's career and his thirst for power. He reminded her almost weekly that *his* sacrifices would pay off once he was a senator. Sacrifices? Dolores never saw him give up anything. In fact, he had a sense of entitlement and acted as though he was impervious to the rules that applied to others.

They had grown apart long ago. Dolores wondered what her life would be like if she simply packed her bags and left. She could take her beloved dog and start a new life for herself. Lord knows she was entitled to half of the money they had in their bank accounts, stocks, and Oliver's secret accounts that were not a secret to her. She could get away from Harrisburg and far away from Oliver.

Rachel's invitation to stay with her sounded very appealing. After all, Rachel's roommate Angela was a neat freak, so the place would be spotless. Angela would never allow wild parties or orgies. The way that Rachel talked about her roommate, she was a bit odd, but nice and quiet. She had an obsessive-compulsive disorder that really controlled her life. *Moving in with two girls that are young enough to be my daughters would not be a becoming image for a mayor's wife, certainly not a senator's wife,* Dolores thought. *A woman should have her own dreams and ambitions,* she pondered.

As it was, her cook would be preparing dinner tonight, Dolores would eat alone, and the staff would retreat for the evening and head home to their simpler worlds. She chose her life with Oliver and knew his aspirations to be in politics when they met. She knew that he had the drive and conviction to do whatever it took to get whatever he wanted. He certainly was not opposed to screwing others to get what he wanted. That thought reminded her again of his most recent infidelity.

A slight smile formed on her lips. Dolores knew at that moment she was ready to move on. She would find a lawyer who was not at her husband's beck and call or on his payroll. Maybe one here in Lancaster. She would divorce him right away, or at least start the process. An apartment of her own would suit her needs. *Something close to the market would be lovely,* she dreamed. And she had plenty of grounds. Or so she thought.

Dolores left the market with Whoopie pies, a beautiful steak, a jar of apple butter made by an Amish family, and her favorite 15-grain bread.

As she began her drive home, Dolores could not wait for her next stop. She had to pick up her ever-faithful Yorkshire Terrier, Muffin.

Nipper's Grooming Salon was convenient for Muffin to get a monthly bath, a trim, and some new bows during Dolores' treasured Friday excursions.

Dolores loved that dog more than anything. The pampered pooch lived the life of a princess and had an attitude equal to a spoiled brat. Those who had the pleasure of being in the company of Muffin soon realized that her four-pound stature, bowed hair and cute face hid a true monster that could only be tamed by Dolores.

The door to Nipper's opened with the sound of a bell that sent the dogs into an ear-piercing, barking fit. The barking sound was deafening to everyone entering the pet salon. For her own sanity purposes, Judy had learned to tune it out years ago.

Judy Preston was the owner of Nippers. Her quaint little pet salon housed three grooming tables. This allowed Judy to schedule grooming appointments with her assistant Jamie. Judy divided her time between grooming and running the day-to-day operations of the salon. She planned to take on one more groomer by spring due to the increasing business.

It had been Judy's dream to expand her services, and after eighteen years of grooming, her dream came true three years prior. She opened her pet salon on East Main Street in the growing town of Mount Joy.

Judy and her husband had purchased a home on Barbara Street when they married right out of high school. He was the star athlete of Donegal High School and she was a business and computer geek. She tutored him in Algebra II and he fell madly in love with her.

Doug went on to become a middle school teacher and she worked for a small company as a computer programmer. His income eventually allowed her to be able to quit her job and to pursue her pet grooming business.

The first fifteen years, she set up shop in their walk-in finished basement. It was a small one-person shop that grew into a thriving business.

Losing her husband had been devastating to Judy and she did not see herself dating anyone else. Even though his death by pancreatic cancer was quick and he did not suffer for a long time, she would always feel like part of her also died that day. Her kind and gentle man could never be replaced.

Outwardly, she appeared to stop grieving, but her heart ached for him every day. The best way that she could honor his memory was to use the money that he left her and become as successful as she could. He would have wanted that for her. "Love what you do and do what you love," he always told her.

Now, three years later, the pet salon was a success. Judy wanted to make sure that it reflected her style while still being functional. The walls were a Pepto-Bismol pink with a gray tiled floor. She always loved that particular shade of pink.

The space was accented with white furniture, towel caddies, grooming tables, and two huge washing stations with hydraulic lifts. Large and small dog crates were placed in several corners with industrial-style dryers pointed at them. Black mats were placed at every workstation to make standing in one place easier for the technicians. The entire set up reminded her of a hair salon.

Retail shelves housed organic dog treats, specialty collars and leashes, cute doggie sweaters and an array of other canine necessities. A picture of a hairy pooch with its tongue hanging out and its head wrapped in a towel with cucumber slices covering its eyes hung between the shelves.

The bell on the door rang. A smile lit Dolores' face when she saw her sweet baby getting a cute bow attached to the top of her tiny adorable head. She failed to see the blood that her sweet angel drew from the grooming assistant's finger. Those sharp teeth could inflict a nasty bite.

The young assistant, Jamie, was gritting her teeth to stop herself from punting the devil dog across the salon. She needed three Band-Aids from this day's visit alone. She threatened worker's comp or combat pay every time she was stuck with the little bitch.

Muffin was Judy's monthly nightmare. She reached for the growling dog from Jamie's grooming table. Judy made the mistake of making eye contact with Jaime before she picked up Muffin. Jamie's murderous glare couldn't be contained.

Judy held the dog away from her body, trying to avoid another bite. The dog latched on to the side of Judy's hand.

Dolores snatched up Muffin. The dog showed her pointy white teeth at Judy, trying desperately to get in another good bite. Muffin was the alpha dog.

Dolores began speaking in a high-pitched baby talk manner that annoyed Judy to no end. She always saw a correlation between her toughest dogs and the way the owners treated them. The more baby talk, the worse the grooming session went for her and her staff. This one put the terror in the terrier.

"Oh, pookie-bear. Momma's gonna take you home and get you some nice beef and rice. Yes, we are, sweetums. You look so pretty with your wittle bows and you smell so lovely, yes you do." Dolores nuzzled her. The dog ate it up. She licked Dolores' face like a child with a lollipop. "Oh, give Momma a kiss, pookie-bear."

It took all of Judy's energy not to vomit. The dog became an innocent baby in Dolores' arms. Not the mean-spirited, pain in the ass she was just two seconds earlier. Muffin's bite was worse than her bark. Judy and her staff had some scars to prove it. However, Dolores was the best tipper and a loyal customer, so Judy tolerated more than her share of doggie abuse.

Dolores thanked Judy, paid her bill, and tipped forty bucks. Judy and Jaime were glad to see her go. Jamie quickly snatched the tip, thinking she needed to start her weekend partying earlier and how many Miller Lights the forty would get her.

Dolores gently placed Muffin into the passenger's seat. Muffin loved patrolling the landscape. Because Dolores hated driving on highways, she always chose to take a much longer, scenic route to Harrisburg. Her route was always the same. She traveled Union School Road and made her way toward the charming town of Marietta. From Marietta, she traveled past Three Mile Island Nuclear Power Plant, through the town of Middletown and onto Route 230 to head toward the Harrisburg Area.

A brisk snow began to fall, causing her to be extra cautious. Dolores decided that maybe she should have forgone her fear of highways, thinking they were probably salted heavily enough to take the paint off of a car. She was not a confident driver and she never liked driving in wet weather of any kind.

The stretch between Marietta and Bainbridge was usually an enjoyable ride because of the absence of high traffic. However, in snowy weather, the lack of drivers or snow plows made the roadway treacherous. Dolores' car crawled from Lancaster County into Dauphin County. As she passed Three Mile Island, Dolores barely glanced at the huge reactors. Instead, she worriedly glanced into her rear-view mirror and noticed a black SUV speeding up behind her. Dolores gripped the steering wheel so hard, the tension traveled up her arms and into her neck and shoulders.

Dolores' tensions mounted with the increasing snow shower. She cautiously slowed her speed to a crawl, hoping the driver behind her would do the same. She rode her brakes the entire way, gripping her steering wheel and wishing she had a chauffeur.

Dolores realized that she was holding her breath, so she let out a cleansing sigh to try to relax a bit. She finally realized that her beloved pooch was whining.

"Oh, pookie-bear, Momma's gonna get us home safely and we will enjoy a lovely treat. Would you like that? Yes, you would, sweetums."

The Yorkie let out a high-pitched bark as if to answer her master, but the whining continued.

Dolores glanced into her mirror again and noticed that the SUV was gaining on her. "Stupid people. Can't they see the roads are terrible? The jerk is going to cause an accident, right, Pookie?" she muttered to her faithful companion.

The SUV was not slowing down. It was rapidly bridging the gap between them. Dolores began to panic. She put on her hazard lights and her eyes were shifting from road to rear view mirror. The SUV was actually starting to pick up speed almost purposefully. Dolores pumped her brakes which sent her back tires sliding. She was hoping to pull over to let the idiot driver pass her. Instead, the SUV slammed into the back of Dolores' Lexus and sent her spinning on the slippery roadway.

Dolores' scream did not have time to escape her mouth before the SUV struck her car again. This time, the impact caused her to veer into a tree.

Muffin was thrown, but escaped serious injury. She began whimpering on the passenger's side floor. Dolores desperately grabbed for her beloved dog, forgetting about her seatbelt. Her head had bounced off the steering wheel and hit the driver's side window. The Lexus's air bags had not engaged. The impact caused her to black out for a moment. Her head was throbbing and her vision blurred. Her hand went to the left side of her head and came back wet and sticky. The sight of her own blood made Dolores queasy. Absentmindedly, she wiped her hand across her coat, as if removing the blood from her hands could erase what had happened. Dolores closed her eyes to the throbbing in her head.

She waited a full minute before she tried to start moving. She twisted her head back and forth and was confident that she did not suffer from a broken neck. She moved down to her shoulders, shrugging them up and relaxing them down. She registered the fact that she maintained feeling in her lower extremities. Dolores said a silent prayer and tried to slow her heart rate.

As she tried to unbuckle her seatbelt to get to Muffin, she noticed someone at her broken window.

"I'm alright, I think," she called out. "I'm alright. I just hit my head, but I think I'm okay."

If she could talk, she was alive, she reasoned, and if she had any broken bones, they would heal.

"Please, help me get out of here. Have you seen my dog? I cannot get to my dog. Help me, please," she pleaded.

She saw the stranger lift their hands and she realized what was about to happen. Her eyes widened. Before she had time to beg for her life, the stranger, without a moment of hesitation, put a bullet through Dolores' skull.

Chapter Two

CHAPTER THREE

Rachel was hoping the rest of the day would be easier than it began. It was not.

Rachel's third client of the day was Jen Islay. She was the wife of Jim Islay. Jim was paralyzed after he ran his motorcycle into a tree. The drunk driving charges against him did not really matter to Jim. After all, it was not as if he was going to be driving any time soon. He paid his fine and slipped into a deep depression from the inability to do most things for himself.

The change in her circumstances, faced with having to be the breadwinner, and her own mental issues took a huge toll on Jen and her level of sanity.

Jen turned to psychic readings, carrying crystals in her purse for positive energy, and anything deemed *alternative*. It was an effort to try to control her moods and calm her nerves. She jumped at any chance to leave the house. Any time the visiting nurse or Jim's family could stay for a few hours, she bolted.

Jen entered the salon with her head down. Her mousy-brown hair was hanging in her depressed-looking face. She was carrying a bunch of hair magazines. She pushed her hair back away from her face, but it fell almost immediately.

Rachel could feel a small headache creeping behind her eyes.

"How are you, Jen?" Rachel tried to sound sincere as she greeted her.

"Horrible. It's snowing again," Jen replied with a deep frown. "Also, my Sagittarius is in sun and my Gemini is in moon, so I'm a mess." Jen slumped into Rachel's chair and began paging through her magazines.

Rachel made eye contact with Valerie, who stopped combing her client's hair at the bizarre comment from Jen Islay. She held her shears in her hand and motioned as if she was stabbing someone.

Rachel's eyes widened to let her friend know that this appointment might be sending her over the edge.

Valerie's snicker earned her an exasperated look from Rachel. Valerie only pointed at the tiara located on her station. The tiara was a salon joke between the three women. Whenever one of them had a difficult client, they earned the tiara and they were named Salon Princess until one of the other women had an even more difficult client. It usually helped to ease the tension. They told the clients that it was because they were the employee of the month. Some of them knew the real reason, and some *were the reason*. Like Jen.

Rachel could not smile back at Valerie at that moment, but she knew her friend would be placing the tiara on her station as soon as she walked away to shampoo Jen's hair. She looked down at the open stylebook on Jen's lap and cleared her throat before entering into what was probably going to be a difficult conversation.

Jen cleared her throat. "Why does it always have to rain or snow when I get my hair done?"

"Yep, this time of year, it snows from time to time." Rachel placed the cape around Jen's neck.

Jen's head was down. She was pouring quickly through one of the hair magazines on her lap.

Rachel knew the sooner she could get started, the sooner she could get Jen's negative energy out of the salon. "So, Jen, what styles are you thinking about today?"

"Well, part of me would like my hair longer. And part of me would like it shorter," Jen began.

Rachel could only nod, realizing that Jen's sun and moon dilemma was going to become this hairstylist's nightmare.

Jen was oblivious and continued her indecisive conversation. "And part of me wants a style that will make my husband think I'm attractive. And another part of me wants *other men* to find me sexy."

Valerie, Shirley and their two clients remained completely silent so that they could listen to Rachel try to interpret the confusing message Jen was giving her.

With a deep breath and slow exhale, Rachel answered. "Well, that's a lot of parts, Jen," Rachel said as sweetly as possible. "Let's look at the styles that you picked in here," she said, grabbing the open magazine located on Jen's lap.

Many pages were dog-eared for reference. Jen took the time to use a black marker to circle each picture that she liked. *It looks like the random markings of a serial killer,* Rachel thought. Every style was different. There was no theme, no care taken in choosing styles that were at least her length. Some models had waist-long hair, some with short spiky hair, and some had shoulder-length hair. Oddly enough, all of them had bangs. Jen never wore her hair toward her face or bangs. She was always pushing her hair away in some sort of feathered, outdated 70s style. Dorothy Hammil's famous hair came to mind.

"I need a change," Jen moaned.

"Well, how about if we stop looking at hairstyles that are actually longer than what you currently have; we could probably eliminate those, right?"

"Yeah, I guess that makes sense." Jen squirmed a little in the chair.

"And in the two years that I have known you, I've never seen you try to spike your hair, so we could safely eliminate that look, too. That would require you to use products to get that look. You hate using products, so would it be safe to eliminate those styles, Jen?"

"Yeah, that makes sense. You remembered I never use products. See that's why I come to you. It's like you can read my mind," said Jen as she stared up at Rachel with a pleading puppy dog look in her eyes.

A snicker from Valerie made it even harder for Rachel to control her own need to laugh.

"So, if you really would like a change, how about we try some light bangs, take two inches off and some soft layers around your face. Would that be alright?"

"You always know what I need," Jen said happily; her mood swaying like a tree in the wind.

Rachel had a sinking feeling that Jen's entire world was riding on one haircut. It was a lot of pressure that women put on their hair stylists' shoulders. Rachel's ability to take control of the situation and interpret her client's needs was one of her strongest attributes.

Shirley smiled at Rachel as she led Jen to the shampoo area. Valerie slipped away from her client and happily placed the tiara on top of Rachel's station.

After the last client left, Shirley, Valerie, and Rachel began to fold the towels in the back room and put them away. Shirley would stop every few seconds to ram some cold fries into her mouth. She lived off fast food and takeout menus. "Val, make sure you leave most of the towels for Rachel to fold. That's punishment for being late again."

Shirley's voice boomed as she spoke and her laugh was an unmistakable cackle that her clients did not seem to mind. Her tone was as big as her figure and her hair; both pushing the limits of acceptability. She kept true to her 80s hairstyle and tight fitting animal-print outfits. Her earrings were always dangling lower than her over-processed, bleached blonde, permed hair.

Shirley spent the first part of her career in New Jersey. Even though she moved to Lancaster, Pennsylvania after she married, the Jersey-girl attitude was still very much alive.

Her clientele was aging, possibly almost deaf, which probably helped muffle the decibels that she gave off. She was also a close talker. Shirley could invade anyone's space without a second thought. And at her size, that was a lot of space. Shirley was an ideal boss, yet she also could grate the nerves at the end of a long day.

Valerie rubbed her temples as Shirley described the phone call she received earlier in the day.

"The man asked if we did massages with happy endings. And I told that fool to come on down here and I'll give him a happy ending. He'll be happy if old Shirley didn't happily serve his limp dick to my dog, Bruno. Ha! Score one for Shirley and zero for the loser looking for cheap thrills. Does the name of my salon remotely sound like we perform those kinds of services? Does Shirley's Hair and Nail Salon sound promiscuous? Ha! I don't think so. Oh, speaking of promiscuous, how was your date with Richard last night, Rachel?"

Rachel stopped folding long enough to glance at Valerie before she addressed her boss. "Wow, Shirl, you don't miss a trick, do ya?" Rachel said, sulking again. "The Dickster got his rocks off and left first thing before I even got up. He just took off."

Valerie threw the morning's half-eaten banana she never got around to finishing into the trash can. "Don't worry about him, Rach, let's go to that new bar, and drown that frown of yours, alright?" Valerie said, pushing her multi-colored hair extensions out of the way. As she swung them, the fuchsia and cobalt blue hairpieces accentuated Valerie's dark hair and blue eyes. "You want to come, Shirley?"

"No, I got to get home and feed Bruno. Oh yeah, and that worthless, Carl wants spaghetti tonight. You girls go. Be safe and do not be late tomorrow. That means you, Rachel."

Rachel rolled her eyes and groaned. "I'm making no promises."

After turning off the lights and locking the salon door, Valerie and Rachel walked the short three blocks to the new contemporary bar, Virgo. The rooms were lightly lit and the bar featured a beautiful waterfall. The water flowed over textured glass. The streamlined furnishings added a nice touch to the bar's sleek architectural atmosphere.

The first thing Rachel thought as she entered the bar was that the air was clean, unlike some other Lancaster bars. Pennsylvania laws were cracking down on smoking in public establishments. Instead of driving away the smoker crowd, restaurant and bar owners had a completely new bar scene and profits were up. If there was a place outside for smokers to go, they would continue to drink. That was where Valerie could be found after every Coors Light.

Rachel sipped on her margarita, careful to lick the salt from the rim of her glass. Her slim build and amazing breasts caught the attention of a few men sitting at the bar. The bartender sent a second margarita to her, compliments of one of her admirers. On a good day, she would have sat up straighter, pushing her chest in their direction and playfully messed with her long red hair. As it was, she was in no mood for any tomfoolery. Well, Tom, Dick or Harry foolery, either. Especially Dick.

Rachel looked around impatiently for Valerie to return from her smoke break. Her eyes locked on a familiar face entering the bar. She witnessed Richard Reynolds strolling in the door. He had a short, slim, blonde-haired woman climbing all over him. She practically wrapped around him like a goddamn Christmas bow.

Rachel was seeing red. She grabbed her fresh drink and held it up. She smiled sweetly at the gentleman who bought it for her and walked over to Richard. His smile changed into an embarrassing glance and then he tried to look away. It was too late. She was coming at him and her deadly glare was enough to tell him trouble was brewing.

Richard started to unravel the blonde-haired woman from his body. "Oh, hey, Rachel! I was going to call you later."

The drink that Rachel threw in his face stopped his words abruptly.

Rachel spun on her heels, went back to the bar, threw a twenty onto the bar to cover the tab, and stormed out the front door. She found Valerie and grabbed her by the arm.

"Hey! I'm busy here!" Valerie complained. She smiled back at the man she was flirting with. "Call me!" Valerie yelled as she struggled to right herself in her four-inch heels.

Richard was just stupid enough to pursue Rachel. After all, he tried for three months to date her, and that date ended amazingly. Very few women had the power to make him unable to walk straight after sex. He quickened his pace toward her with the blonde clattering behind him in her too-high heels and her too-short skirt.

"Oh, come on, Rachel, stop! It's not as if we're a couple or anything. It was just one great night. One *really* great night." He had caught up and stood blocking Rachel's path as she turned away from him.

"I was hoping that we could, you know, hang out again sometime." His shitty grin was the last straw for Rachel.

"Ignore him, Rachel, and keep walking," Valerie advised as she started pulling on Rachel's arm. Rachel could not control her anger and turned to stand directly in front of Richard. She faked a sweet smile. "You know, Richard, maybe we should hang out again," she said sarcastically.

"Yeah, like I was saying; hang out and..."

Rachel interrupted. "But only after you fix this!" she said as she kneed him in the groin as hard as she could.

Richard grunted and he hit the pavement. He was curled into a fetal position, holding his balls and swearing through his incredible pain.

"I'll kill you, Rachel! Damn it, woman, I'll kill you for this!" he managed to bellow through the agony. He vomited all over the sidewalk, dangerously close to the blonde-haired woman's shoes.

Rachel turned to the woman. "You might wanna rethink your plans for this evening. I think Richard is pretty much out of commission for the night. Maybe for the rest of the month. I just did you a favor. Puke-boy will not be getting it up any time soon. Even if he did manage to sleep with you, he would leave before you woke up and put his business card on your dresser like some cheap whore," she said, patting the blonde on the shoulder.

"He did that to you?" the blonde asked.

"Just last night."

"But he told me that he wasn't with anyone in a long time."

Valerie chuckled. "Less than twenty-four hours is a long time for him." That's why we call him the Dickster."

The woman turned and kicked Richard in the stomach. She turned, hailed a cab, then she was gone.

Rachel swung around to face Valerie. She was giggling at the scene of Richard rolling on the ground, trying to miss the vomit. She nudged Rachel's arm. "He went before you got up and left you his business card? No wonder you were pissed. That is just tacky. But was the sex good?" Valerie put her arm around her friend and they turned from the scene.

They walked arm in arm, Rachel smiling and Valerie drawing attention with her ever-provocative swagger. "Unfortunately, it was pretty good. A real man does not treat you like he just paid you for your services. It cheapens everything, and come to think of it, he did make some weird sound at the end."

"Weird sound?"

"Yeah, like Homer Simpson. 'D'oh'. You know how he always says that."

Valerie laughed so hard, she had to stop herself from doubling over in pain.

"Seriously? He is now named Homer Simpson! Oh my gosh, that's too much!"

Rachel started to laugh as well. "D'oh! I guess he'll be out of commission for a while," boasted Rachel.

"Yeah, what happened in there?" Valerie questioned as she searched in her coat pocket for her lip-gloss.

"Didn't you see him walk in with the blonde?" Rachel shoved her gloved hands into her coat pockets.

Valerie gave her friend a sheepish look. "No, I was, uh, distracted. But I did catch what he had for lunch. That was disgusting!"

"Yeah, I saw that you were distracted. What's his name?"

"Randy, something or other."

"Something or other?" Rachel shook her head. "Is that German or Irish?"

"Rach, I didn't really care about the name. Did you see those pecs, those amazing arms, holy shit." Valerie applied a second coat of lip-gloss to her lips and shoved the tube back into her pocket. "I was a little busy admiring that body and trying to make first contact."

"First contact? Christ, Val! You sound like you just met an alien. That's it, no more Star Trek for you."

"First contact is the flirt and the passing of phone numbers, you know—the digits. The second contact is the first phone call and getting a date. I am sure I do not need to explain the third and fourth contact to you. He was *not an alien*, he was a god!"

Rachel let out a giggle as she flipped her long locks out of her face. "Well, let's wait and see if *Randy the God* calls you back. Do you even have anything in common or is that a stupid question?"

Valerie opened her purse and began searching for her house key. "Well, my new plan is to pick up men in the smoking section. That way I know right away that they are not smoking haters. Pretty clever right?"

"Good plan, Val," Rachel answered distractedly. "So far you have smoking in common, that's a start." Rachel's comment was half-hearted. "A longtime relationship made from the love of nicotine. It should last forever, as long as one of you doesn't decide to get healthy and quit."

"Quit? I am no quitter. When I commit to something, I commit," Valerie teased. "Anyway, I have the lungs of a forty-year-old."

"Too bad you're only twenty-five." Rachel shivered loudly.

"Let's just get out of the snow. I got some Fudgy Pudgy ice cream in the freezer and we'll order Chinese. You can crash at my place. I'm sure your weird roommate won't mind."

"Oh, she'll be calling to see when I am coming home so that she can put the door lock off her list of things that she has to check before she can go to bed. She is peculiar like that. I have never seen anything like it. She wants to know where I am and when I will be home."

"I know, she's got that Single White Female thing going on. She is obsessed with your comings and goings. It's just creepy." Valerie faked a shiver at the thought of Angela and her weird ways.

"Angela means well. She's just an introvert." Rachel always had the urge to defend Angela. She had a feeling Valerie was a little jealous that she, Rachel, chose to live with Angela and not Valerie.

Valerie took the conversation to another level. "No, she just wants to get into your pants. She also has that Attention Deficit thingy."

"Gross, Val! Stop saying shit like that! She is not trying to sleep with me. You're starting to annoy me."

Valerie knew she could taunt Rachel even more and it was fun to see her friend get peeved. "Hey, with the rack you have, it's no wonder. I'd do you, but I like the male anatomy way too much," Valerie teased.

Rachel just laughed. She knew her friend was trying to get a rise out of her and was in no way attracted to the same sex.

The girls walked up the stairs to Valerie's apartment building. Rachel was almost run over by a handsome man who was running out of the building. He stopped when he saw who he just ran into. It was the sweet Rachel Perry, the goddess of his dreams. What he would give to spend a few hours with her.

"Oh, hello, Taz," Valerie began to smile that provocative smile that she knew was killer to most men. Somehow, though, it never seemed to work on her neighbor, Taz. "Are you heading to the hospital? I barely get to see you now that they put you on the night shift," Valerie pouted.

"Yep, interns always get the shit shifts," he answered, barely taking his eyes off of Rachel, who was starting to rub her hands together and dancing up and down from the cold.

Taz felt deflated that Rachel barely seemed to notice him. It was not as if he was not fit, because he was a regular at the gym. Other women found him attractive. Not that he could count the flirting from Valerie; she would flirt with a corpse. The thought of a corpse brought him back to reality. "I'm late! Sorry ladies, I got to fly!"

Taz took off running down the street to his car. Valerie stopped by the front door of her building to stare in his direction. "Sweet Mary, he's hot. Don't you think so, Rach?"

"He's not really my type. His arms look like bags of meat. And he has no neck."

"That's because he has all those gorgeous muscles. Necks are overrated. Who needs a neck anyway?"

"Well it does keep your head on straight, so, it's kind of important. Will you please just open the door, Val? I'm freezing!"

Valerie unlocked the door, and both girls knocked the snow off their shoes as they walked into Valerie's apartment. They peeled off the layers of winter wear. Coats, scarves, gloves littered the chair near the door.

The apartment was cozy and warm. Soft beige colors and well-worn neutral furniture, created an inviting and welcoming environment.

"Man, is it cold out there or what?" Valerie shivered as she looked for her phone in her messy purse. "I wish that one of us had a car so that we could get around better. There is nothing worse than getting snow in your pumps."

Rachel yawned aloud. "That's why I love my boots. Keep your feet dry and they look so good with everything. Yeah, a car would help with all of the running back and forth we do."

"You know we could make this easier and you could just move in here with me," offered Valerie as she searched her phone for the number to the Chinese restaurant.

They had *the conversation* at least monthly about Rachel moving in. "No, thanks. With the ever-revolving door of your love life, I would become a little depressed."

"Oh, stop. It's not *that* great," Valerie countered.

"Are you kidding, Val? You're in love every other week."

"That's an exaggeration. Look how long I dated Evan. Three months! I only broke up with him when I found out he was addicted to porn and he used my credit card to pay for it. I'm still making payments from that bastard."

Valerie began to mess with her phone and Rachel helped herself to a few Hershey Kisses from the candy dish on the coffee table. She arranged the silver wrappers into a nice neat aluminum pile.

"Val, explain to me why a guy that you know for three short months has access to your credit cards."

"We were in love. He moved in and everything."

"Evan was a douche-bag and moved in to free load off you. He had no job."

"He was an artist."

"Again, he had no job. He just ate your food, ran up your bills, watched porn while you worked and then he left you with a huge debt. A huge porn debt at that! Did you actually ever see him paint anything?"

"Um, no. He said he had a painter's block. That's something that creative people have to deal with."

"Ever see a canvas or paints? How about watercolors? Did he even own a damn crayon?"

Valerie paused. "Well, when you put it that way, he wasn't much of an artist."

"He wasn't an artist at all!" Rachel said with an exasperated sigh.

She rummaged through the freezer to find their favorite ice cream. She found two clean spoons and plopped onto the haggard sofa. One of the springs poked out as she landed and stuck Rachel in her backside. She quickly jumped up. "Ouch! Damn it, Val! Your stupid couch just stuck me in the ass again!"

Valerie let out a hearty laugh and just shook her head as she dialed her phone to place their order. "Hey, I've had that couch since I was eighteen. It is the only constant thing in my life."

"Oh?" Rachel said, lifting her brow toward her friend as she carefully sat down again without any further poking.

"Well, except for you."

"I was going to say," Rachel teased.

Val placed the order, hung up and plopped next to Rachel on the couch without incident.

"See, you just have to know where to plant your ass."

"Seriously, Val, you should consider replacing this old, stained-up beast with something pretty. Maybe something in animal-print; that would go great with the clay and beige colors on your walls and the exposed brick."

"Tempting."

"Hell, I'd even pitch in for it, due to the amount of time I spend here."

"Again, tempting. But until I pay off the porn, I can barely make my rent."

"That sounds so weird when you say it that way," Rachel said, digging into the ice cream. The stress of the day made it impossible to wait for dinner to arrive.

"Hey, save some for me!" Valerie said, slapping Rachel on the arm.

"Ouch! Sorry, I guess I am inhaling this a little too fast."

"Ya think?" pouted Valerie as she grabbed the ice cream container and shoved a giant-sized spoonful into her mouth.

After a satisfying amount of chicken fried rice, the two women settled in for a Julia Roberts-starring chick flick and the rest of the ice cream. Rachel reached for a fortune cookie and broke it open, scattering crumbs on herself and the couch.

"Let's see what my fortune says. All right, it says *wealth and happiness will find you.*"

"In bed," answered Val.

"What?" questioned Rachel.

"Remember, you always add the phrase, *in bed* to your fortune. Wealth and happiness will find you in bed." Valerie said with a giggle. "That's a good one. Are you sure you didn't open mine?"

"Nope, it was closest to me. It's mine."

"So, you are going to be rich and happy. What are you going to do, play the Pennsylvania Lottery tomorrow?"

"Maybe I should. It's up to twenty-five million. The first thing I'm going to buy is a new couch for you!" Rachel said, glancing at Valerie.

"Sweet! Can you also pay off some porn? That would be fabulous!"

"You're pushing it," Rachel answered with a yawn. "Hey, I'm ready to turn in."

Chapter THREE

"Me, too," answered Valerie.

Both women always shared Valerie's king-sized bed. Rachel insisted on new sheets, not trusting her friend to change them after a night of fun. Valerie set the alarm as Rachel brushed her teeth and changed into sweats and a tee. Rachel kept plenty of spare clothing and beauty items at Valerie's apartment. She never knew when Valerie would talk her into spending the night. They both fell asleep to the sound of the television, oblivious to the rest of the world.

CHAPTER
FOUR

W here is she? Where in heaven-sake is she?" Angela Wright wondered aloud. She was getting ready for bed and had no clue if her roommate, Rachel Perry was alright or dead in a ditch somewhere.

She carefully brushed and flossed her teeth. Her OCD symptoms made her count the number of strokes of the toothbrush.

She ignored the tell-tale signs of the disorder in her dry, chapped hands. Her obsessive hand washing was not a huge concern for her. She took the meds her shrink had recommended. It was just a little something to take the anxiety off. That is what her shrink had said.

Well, it was not working anymore, Angela thought to herself. She refused to up her dose like the doctor suggested. It made her feel zoned out and not in control. However, her symptoms were growing at an alarming pace ever since she decided to room with her old classmate, Rachel Perry.

Angela suddenly flew out of the bathroom in a panic, thinking for the third time that she needed to check the apartment door lock. She locked and unlocked several times to be sure.

She decided to make her regular scan of the apartment. Angela checked Rachel's room. The mess sent her reeling. Jeans and blouses were haphazardly hung on mismatched hangers. Some plastic, some wire, some from the stores where she bought her clothes. Nothing was coordinated. The mountain of heels and boots seemed to grow weekly and there was something sticking out of her dresser drawer, where it appeared that Rachel shut the drawer without securing the items first.

Ick! How could anyone live like that? she wondered. Rachel hid it well before Angela decided to rent one of her spare bedrooms. If she would have known about Rachel's sloppy manners, she might have declined, even though the rent was cheap.

Angela checked her empty bedroom. Nothing was out of order. She marched into the living room. Nothing seemed out of place except the cushions on the sofa. She quickly realigned them. The fringed leopard rug in front of the sofa drove her nuts. Rachel refused to replace it with a sensible, non-fringed variety. Angela combed her fingers over the fringes to straighten them and continued on to the apartment door again.

Angela knew that because Rachel was not in the apartment, she could not place the chain lock in its place. That really bugged her. Instead, she locked and unlocked the deadbolt several more times. *One, two, three, four, five to six and now, it is fixed,* she chanted in her head.

She pulled on the door a few times until she was satisfied that it was locked.

She sauntered into the kitchen. The sink was clean and dry; no water spots were ever tolerated. All of the dishes were in their rightful places and the counters were pristine. Angela knew to focus on things she could control.

Satisfied that everything was in order, Angela returned to her own bedroom.

She sat on the edge of her bed and, removing her hairbrush from the bedside table drawer, she began taking out her frustration on her hair.

She could not tell if it was the stress of her disorder, the stress of living with Rachel, or maybe she had something new to worry about. Like maybe, her thyroid was not working because of her meds. Angela knew that if she kept with that train of thought, she would never get to sleep. She knew that when and if Rachel came home, she would have to reexamine the front door because she could not count on Rachel to lock the door and it really irritated her. The abuse of the hair continued until Angela began to panic that maybe she was brushing so hard that she was causing bald spots. She gasped at the amount of hair in her brush and threw it into the drawer. She had to take it out and clean it thoroughly because keeping the hair in the brush was disgusting. Her mind raced as she pulled the hair from the brush and placed it into the trash can in the bathroom. She knew that first thing tomorrow, she would have to empty it properly. Living with Rachel was making her crazy.

Rachel is so irresponsible. She should at least let someone know if she wasn't coming home, she muttered.

Angela changed her clothes and carefully folded down her crisp, white sheets. She found her reading glasses and picked up her huge copy of *North and South*. She found her place and began to read. Reading always calmed her. It allowed her to visit someone else's life and escape her mind.

"Focus on something. Like a movie or a good book," her doctor had advised. It always worked and within half an hour, her eyes began to droop.

She faintly heard a sound at the apartment door and the sound of that annoying floorboard creaking that always drove her nuts.

Angela was secretly relieved that Rachel finally found her way home and after she knew that Rachel was in her room, she could check the door again.

The footsteps stopped just outside of her bedroom door, but Angela was in no mood to talk to Rachel about not calling again, so she placed her book on the bedside table, shut off her light, and rolled away from the door. She forgot to lock her bedroom door and heard the door open slightly. She thought Rachel must have seen the light from under the door and knew she was still awake. Still, she remained silent and kept her lights off.

Someone was standing in the doorway. They moved to stand close to the bed. Angela was not in the mood to listen to Rachel's excuses. "Go away, Rac…" was all she could say before her sentence was stopped by the bullet that pierced the back of her head.

CHAPTER FIVE

"Rachel, get up!" Valerie yelled from the bathroom. "You're going to make us late again."

"Err, just five more minutes, Mommy," Rachel answered groggily. She sat up, rubbing her eyes and yawning profusely. "Val, I know why you can't keep a guy. You snore excessively loud. You kept me up half the night," she said as she pulled the covers to the side and sat on the edge of the bed.

"Hey, no personal attacks before breakfast. Get up and we'll stop at the café on our way." Valerie was pulling on her tight jeans and shoving on her boots. Her denim shirt was tied at the waist and barely buttoned to hide her cleavage. She impatiently combed through her hair as she applied her makeup. A true multi-tasker.

Rachel took her time. "Just let me focus a minute. Hell, it's only 7:30; we have plenty of time. I'll just jump in the shower and be out in a jiffy," Rachel said, sliding off the bed and tiptoeing across the cold, wooden floor.

"Famous last words," muttered Valerie. She knew it never ended well when Rachel was *done in a jiffy.*

Thirty minutes later, Rachel emerged from the bathroom. Her black pants were a staple in her hair stylist wardrobe and she always kept at least one pair at Valerie's. She was careful to never spend too much on work clothes. Murphy's Law would always be proven right every time she slopped color on her brand-new shirt, or bleach on her black pants. It was the never-ending struggle of a hairstylist. She rummaged through her purse until she found her black Magic Marker and touched up a small bleach spot on her pants. The beauty school trick had stuck with her. *Beats buying new pants.*

Valerie practically shoved Rachel out of the door and locked it behind herself. The girls walked as fast as they could down the street toward the café. Some of the residents did not clear off the snow on their sidewalks from the previous night, so it made their walk a little treacherous.

When they entered their favorite morning hangout, Valerie noticed someone familiar.

"Hey, Rach, that's the guy who was in the salon the other day. Remember? You were with Dolores and I was, uh taking my time cutting his hair. He was quiet, but just look at those eyes. They are dark and mysterious. That's just what I need right now, a little mystery."

Val was tossing her hair, trying to get his attention. He silently continued to read his newspaper, seemingly oblivious to her.

"Val, would you give it a rest. It's too early to watch you trying to score," Rachel said, rubbing her eyes.

"Oh, it's never too early to score. I am always up for a challenge. Check out his full head of hair. I admit to running my fingers through it more than I had to the other day," Valerie answered with a toss of her long, multi-colored hair. She reached in her pocket for her lipgloss and carefully applied another layer. "I'm going to go and say hi," Valerie said as she rose from her chair.

"How do you know he'll remember you?" Rachel questioned.

"Hmmm, how could he not," Valerie replied over her shoulder with a grin. She approached the man with a seductive swagger and practically ran into Taz, who just finished his shift at the hospital and went to the coffee shop hoping that he would run into Rachel on her way to work. "Morning, Rachel, you are looking gorgeous as usual."

"Morning, Taz. Thanks, I feel half put together. Valerie practically dragged me out of the apartment. We're not even late. Being early is overrated anyway. Rough night at the hospital?"

"Oh, the usual. Drug-overdose, two pregnant women in labor. Oh, there was one person they brought in on a stretcher. He was swearing about some bitch, his word not mine, who kneed him in the groin outside of that new bar, you know the one I'm talkin' about?"

Rachel felt her face flush. "Yeah, I'm familiar with the place." She sunk a little in her chair and took another sip of coffee as she listened to Taz ramble on, knowing that he was talking about Richard.

"Well, he was saying that he was going to get her good for breaking his balls."

"Huh." Rachel's attention swayed to Valerie. She sat back and watched the pro. Valerie leaned forward to give him a great view of her cleavage. She always dressed for just such an occasion. Valerie was the master of sexuality.

The stranger smiled up at her and engaged her in a conversation. Valerie was pouring it on thick. She returned to the table after a few minutes. Her face was beaming. She slid into her chair with a renewed cheerfulness. She blew out a breath and closed her eyes. Her hand started fanning her face. "Man, he's a hot one. Is it hot in here?"

"It's just your raging hormones heating up the place." Rachel smiled at her friend's antics as Taz slid into the chair next to Rachel's.

"Oh no, John is amazing. Those dark mysterious eyes, his killer build. Oh, hey, Taz!"

Valerie appeared flushed and ready for a romp with the mysterious man.

"Yeah, yeah, did you get a last name this time?" Rachel's sarcasm did not go unnoticed.

"Yes, smart-ass, I got a last name. It's Smith."

Rachel began to chuckle and choked on her coffee. "Smith?" She jabbed Taz in the ribs. He was laughing so hard at Valerie, it made Rachel laugh even more.

"What's so funny about Smith? It's a very normal name."

"Val, John Smith? Really? Come on, he made it up. I would bet fifty bucks that is not his real name. He's blowing you off," Rachel said, wiping at her mascara.

"If anyone's going to be blowing..."

"Not funny, don't even finish that thought. It is too early for your dirty humor," Taz joined in.

Valerie suddenly looked at her watch. "Shit! Damn it, Rach, you made us late again."

"I made us late? I'm not the one trying to score before 9:00." Rachel grabbed her purse and swung it over her shoulder. "See ya, Taz," she said over her shoulder, almost forgetting her coffee.

Both women grabbed their to-go cups and bolted out the door. Taz was left sitting alone and regretting another lost opportunity to ask Rachel out on a date.

Rachel and Valerie ran as fast as they could. "I made us late? You're the one who had to stop for Mr. Fake Name," Rachel huffed while trying not to spill her coffee.

"Oh, whatever, let's just get there, okay?" Val answered, trying not to trip on the slick, icy sidewalks.

They arrived at the salon just as Shirley was turning on the open sign. "Alright, what part of fifteen minutes early don't you get, Rachel Perry?" Shirley perched her large hands on her even larger hips.

"Why is it always me?"

"Because you're always late, girl. You know you are, Rachel. I didn't hire you for your timeliness, that's for sure."

"Always is a strong word, Shirl," was Rachel's rebuttal as she made her way to the back room. She threw her handbag in its usual place on the floor and began making coffee. Valerie entered the back room, chewing on her coffee shop bagel.

"Ya know, the café can rock out some mean bagels. Want some?" she offered, putting her bagel out for Rachel to take a bite.

"You know I don't do breakfast," Rachel muttered. "Just coffee."

"Hey, want to order pizza today? Remember how cute the delivery boy was from Rufffano's?"

"I didn't like the huge gap between his teeth."

"Minor details, minor details."

"I guess I'm picky," Rachel countered with a shrug. "Pizza works. Maybe Shirley will buy it this time."

"Don't count on it. You were late again. You should buy the pie."

"You were with me, Val, and just as late."

Shirley entered the back room, heaving a large laundry basket full of towels and capes. "Do you two think I don't know you hide this laundry? Start some more laundry," Shirley said, shoving the basket at Valerie.

"How do you know it's me?"

"This came from the hamper next to your station, Einstein," Shirley said, leaving the room.

"Oh, I was going to get that anyway." Valerie backed down. She began sorting the colored towels and making several piles. She dumped the whites into the machine and threw in some soap and bleach. She turned on the washing machine and slammed the door. "Is it just me, or is Shirl bitchy today?" Valerie said to Rachel, who was pouring coffee into a carafe to serve to the morning customers.

"Well, maybe she and Carl had another fight. If he would just get his lazy ass off the sofa and get a job or at least help her around the house, then he might stand a chance. Otherwise, she's going to take his head off."

"Rachel, get out here!" Shirley yelled. "Hurry up! You gotta see this!"

The yelling from Shirley stunned both Rachel and Valerie. The non-typical behavior sent the girls running.

"Come here, come here! Oh my God, look!"

Rachel and Valerie quickly went to see what all the fuss was about.

"Look," Shirley said, placing an arm over Rachel's shoulder as she stared at the television.

Rachel began to watch, unclear as to what the issue was. She tried to focus on what the reporter was saying,

"Police are currently ruling her death as an accident. There has been a statement from the Mayor's office. We'll take you to where a spokesperson for the Mayor' will be making a statement."

The scene on the television changed to the Mayor's office. A man in a suit began reading a statement from a note card. "Good Morning. Yesterday afternoon, there was a terrible traffic accident that involved Mayor Harrison's wife, Dolores Harrison. Mrs. Harrison was traveling on Route 441 outside of Middletown. Her car apparently, slid out of control on the slippery roadway. So far, no witnesses have come forward. Anyone with any information, please contact the

Police Department. There will be a candlelight vigil tonight, outside of the Capitol building.

The scene changed back to the reporter. "Mayor Harrison is said to be mourning in his home, surrounded by loved ones and close friends His son, Nicholas Harrison, was seen earlier arriving at the Mayor's home."

Rachel's hand went to her mouth. Tears began to sting her eyes. Her body began to tremble as sobs raked her to the core. "Dead? How is that possible? I just saw her. I just saw her."

Valerie knew how close Dolores and Rachel were and she came to her friend, hugging her close, consoling her as best she could. Hot tears ran down Rachel's face as she shook her head in bewilderment. "Oh my God, I just saw her yesterday," Rachel sobbed, wiping her nose with the back of her hand.

Valerie hugged her friend even tighter. "I know, honey. She was very special to you. I don't know what to say. I'm here for you, Rachel."

Rachel pulled away from Valerie to look at Shirley. "I gotta go. I cannot stay today. Please, Shirley, I gotta go."

Shirley grabbed Rachel's hand. "We have you covered. Go. You need to take a few days, I understand," whispered Shirley as she grabbed and hugged Rachel. She snatched a tissue and wiped Rachel's tear-stained cheeks.

"Do you want me to go with you?" Valerie offered.

"No, please take care of my clients. If you can't fit them in, can you move them to next week? I just need to be alone," Rachel answered. She distanced herself from her co-workers.

Rachel went to get her things out of the back room and left the salon. She walked the few blocks to her apartment and was grateful that Angela would be at work. Rachel wanted some time to digest what she had just learned. Shock was an understatement. She could not feel, she could not think. The last time she saw Dolores, she was heartbroken about finding out that her husband was having an affair. She reached into her purse and felt the little book that Dolores entrusted to her and began to sob even more. It was like losing a mother and friend all at the same time.

As she walked down Orange Street, the snow began to fall again. Rachel hurried her steps, longing for the safety and warmth of her bed. She entered her apartment building and went straight into the elevator. She pressed the third-floor button and waited for the elevator door to close. The elevator was a constant source of agony for Rachel because of how slow it ran. She repeatedly pressed the close button and wiped her nose again. Tears were streaming down her cheeks but she fought back an urge to cry aloud.

The door slowly closed and the elevator traveled to the third floor. The doors opened and Rachel exited and made a right turn toward her apartment, number 317. As she approached the door, the hot tears felt as if they could burned her cheeks and she felt like she couldn't breathe. A full-on panic attack was not what she needed.

Rachel unlocked the door and stood in the doorway with her eyes closed and she sobbed. When she opened her eyes, the sight of her apartment caught her off guard. The entire living room was trashed. Pillows were shredded, white stuffing spewed onto the floor. Her couch cushions were thrown across the room and gutted, her desk was completely filled with papers from the desk drawers. Even her kitchen was a mess. All of her cabinets were emptied; glasses and dishes broken. Rachel stood in disbelief and fear that whomever did this was still in her apartment. She was unable to move for a few seconds.

Her eyes began to slowly scan the rest of the apartment. Her senses immediately fixed on Angela's bedroom door. The door was ajar. She knew Angela would never leave her bedroom door open—not ever. Angela would have made sure the door was shut before leaving for work. She concluded that whomever broke into the apartment and ransacked her place must have also been in Angela's room.

God, she's gonna be pissed when she sees this mess, thought Rachel.

New feelings filled Rachel; feelings of fear and disbelief. She slowly made her way to Angela's bedroom door. "Angie, are you here? Ang…" The rest caught in her throat as she opened the door. Angela's white, pristine bed was covered in blood. The wall she had been facing contained sprayed brain matter and dried blood that had run down the ivory surface. Bright red seemed to cover the entire room, which was usually void of all color. There, lying with her face away from the door was Rachel's roommate. Her blood covered her hair and pillow. Someone had shot her in the head.

Rachel let out a blood-curdling scream. She ran out of the apartment. Her hands were shaking as she reached into her coat pocket for her phone. She raced down the back steps, trying to get as much distance between her and the scene in her apartment. She went out the front door, stood next to the front of the building, and dialed 911. Rachel's body slid down the wall as she passed out.

Rachel regained consciousness when she felt someone was tapping on her cheek. She was propped against the wall, outside her apartment. A small crowd was gathering nearby. Her neighbors were trying to get a glimpse of Rachel. She could hear them begin to gossip.

Rachel felt her cheeks flush at the attention she was drawing. She saw the lights and heard sirens approaching. There was an ambulance and people in uniforms talking in a small circle to her left. Her head was swimming and she felt as though she was going to faint again. As things began to go black, she heard a woman's voice and felt a light tap on her cheek again.

"Miss Perry, come on now, wake up. Miss Perry, can you hear me?" The female police officer continued to try to wake Rachel. Rachel groaned as she began to come to for a second time. "Mmm, what happened?"

"You fainted, Miss Perry. Please sit up and tell me what happened."

Rachel sat up and the reality of what she had seen began to hit her again. Her shaking hands flew up to her mouth. "Angela, oh my… Angela. First Dolores and now Angela. What is going on? Why are people around me dying? I went in and… and is she, is she dead? She's dead. Oh no, oh!" Rachel began to sob again, her mascara running down her cheeks. She rubbed her nose with the sleeve. "No, they are both dead! Her body was shaking and her stomach was flipping repeatedly. Her mouth started to water and she swallowed hard. The last thing she wanted to do was vomit on the sidewalk in front of all her nosy neighbors.

"I'm afraid so. Miss Perry, are you aware of anyone who would want to hurt Miss Wright? How long have you known her? Who else are you talking about? Is there someone else dead?"

Rachel could barely comprehend everything the police officer was asking her. Of course there was someone else. Didn't the police know that Dolores died too?

She was pale and her stomach was queasy. Bile burned her throat. Rachel swallowed hard, trying to fight the urge to vomit. The more she thought about the blood in Angela's bed and on the walls, the worse it got. Waves of nausea plagued her. She could not get the image of Angela with her head blown apart out of her mind. It was too much. Rachel suddenly sat forward, unable to swallow anymore, and turned to the side, vomited all over the shoes of the man standing next to her.

Rachel looked up with embarrassment flushing her pale face. Remnants of bile clung to her chin. She looked up and was met by the steel-gray eyes of a stern-looking man.

Gordan Ryan had enough of the women's drama for the day. Unfortunately, his day was just beginning. "Well, now that we've established her inability to handle crime scenes, I'm just going to go over here to the corner and clean off this mess. After which, I will be taking Miss Perry into my custody," said the remarkably handsome man with vomit on his shoes.

The female cop, Michelle Kinsley stood and walked over to face Gordon's glare. "This has nothing to do with the FBI, Gordon. This is a case for our Criminal Investigation division; not the damn FBI. You have no jurisdiction here."

"Oh, but I do, Mickey, the FBI has jurisdiction over everything, when it involves a government office."

"What government office? This is a murder investigation of a young woman with no government ties. It has nothing to do with you or your office."

Agent Gordon Ryan was losing what patience he thought he had left. He usually did when dealing with his ex-girlfriend, Michelle. However, it gave him a great amount of satisfaction to get under her skin and pull rank on her.

Michelle Kinsley hated the nickname Mickey. She had hated it ever since she was a little girl and her mother and father would call her Mickey. The kids at school called her Mouse and would throw cheese at her in the cafeteria. At some point, she thought she should have outgrown the nickname, but her parents never stopped calling her Mickey. Gordon knew she hated it, which was why he was using it. The bastard never stopped finding ways to annoy her.

She liked to pretend their breakup was mutual. She thought she should move on when she slept with his friend, Gary and some other cops in neighboring communities. He agreed.

The tension and unresolved anger had them pissing each other off like a choreographed dance. He moved, she moved. He yelled, she yelled louder. She moved out of his apartment three years earlier. She moved on from him, from Gary, and started seeing someone not in law enforcement. Gordon was still harboring a huge grudge and she saw no way around that. Three years later, they still hated each other. Him because she cheated. Her because she just damn well felt like hating him.

Michelle swung away from Gordon and turned her attention back to Rachel, who was holding her head, wiping her chin and sobbing softly.

"Miss Perry, I would like you to come with me and give a formal statement." Michelle did not bother to look in Gordon's direction, but she knew there would be an objection coming. Gordon did not waste any time in giving it.

"Miss Perry, you will be coming with me," he stated. His murderous glare sucked something out of Michelle. She visibly wilted before his next clipped words were uttered.

"Don't even try to fight me on this, Mickey. I have the paperwork to prove it. This is our case now and your commanding officer knows it. The FBI is taking this one. You do not need to know any more than that. Go check with your boss if you wish to. I will escort Miss Perry out of here."

She began to argue, but he cut her off quickly. "No buts, I've said enough," Gordon all but shouted. The woman was getting on his last nerve.

Michelle's face showed just how furious she became over his smugness.

"Let's not make a scene here, Mickey. You know damn well I'll win," the handsome FBI Agent answered. "I always do."

The female cop stood and moved in closer to Gordon Ryan, her face almost touching his. They glared at each other for several seconds then she sneered. "You really need to let the past go!"

"It's been gone for a very long time, *Mickey*," Gordon said dispassionately.

Rachel needed a distraction from the thoughts of her room-mate and started to focus on the conversation going on between the two law enforcement personnel in front of her. They were fighting over which person was taking her in. In where? She was not going anywhere with either one of them. Were they blaming her for what happened to Angela? She knew there was no way that anyone who knew her could pin a murder on her. She could barely kill a spider. And the last thing she wanted to become was a yo-yo between these two. She was used to dealing with others and was an excellent judge of people.

In the short time she sat there listening to the two of them bickering, she knew they had some kind of history that apparently did not end very well.

Michelle stalked away and disappeared into the building. Gordon began to look for something to clean off his shoes.

Rachel felt guilty about the mess and she pulled a used tissue out of her large purse and handed it to him. He reluctantly took it and tried to remove the vomit before it dried.

"Uh, thanks," he managed to murmur as he wiped his shoes.

"Hey, I'm sorry about the shoes."

She looked pathetic with her tear-stained cheeks and with black mascara running down her face. Her hands were shaking and her bottom lip was quivering as if she was going to have another break-down at any moment. Gordon was not heartless and he pitied the woman. He was sure under that smeared mess was a pretty girl that probably was not strong enough to handle what she was going to have to face in the next few days. He needed her head in the game so that he could solve the crime quickly and distance himself from her, his ex, Michelle, and the pressure he would get from his boss if things took too long.

Gordon threw the used tissue into the nearby trash can by the parking meter before turning to address her apology. "Yeah, well it's alright. Most of it came off. I don't know many people that have a stomach for this sort of thing that don't deal with it on a regular basis." He tried to sound sincere.

"Well, even if I did see this all the time, I don't think I could get used to it. I'd have nightmares or something," Rachel replied as she stood and found her footing. Still feeling flush and a little light headed, she managed to lean against the wall. "Uh, what do I call you? Are you a detective, an officer or what?"

"Agent Gordon Ryan," he said, displaying his badge. "I'm going to need you to come with me, Miss Perry."

"It's Rachel. I am not going anywhere with anyone. Since I obviously cannot go home, I'm not sure where I'll go. Probably Val's apartment. But I do know it's not going to be with the police. I need some space to make sense of this. So, if you'll excuse me, I'm out of here." Rachel tried to walk toward the street corner, but Gordon blocked her way.

"Miss Perry, it is for your own good that you cooperate," he said, grabbing a hold of her arm.

"Again, it's Rachel, and it would be for your own good to let go of my arm," Rachel said, not at all intimidated by the agent's six-foot stature.

"Alright, Miss Perry, we'll do this the hard way," Agent Ryan said, reaching for his handcuffs. He grabbed her arms and forced her hands behind her back. He handcuffed her before she could protest.

Rachel's neighbors were getting the show they wanted. Some gasped, others nodded as if they expected she would end up a hardened criminal some day.

"You have the right to remain silent."

"Hey! Wait a minute! Rachel interrupted. "What the hell do you think you're doing?" Rachel was pissed and embarrassed. "Get these off of me!" She struggled against the handcuffs.

She began to yell and tried to shrug the agent off of her.

Gordon was not deterred. He continued to recite the Miranda Rights to her. He only answered her after he was finished. "Like I said, we'll do this the easy way or the hard way. It makes no difference to me. I'm sure you don't want to add resisting arrest, do you?" Agent Ryan began to shove Rachel toward the curb.

Rachel tried planting her feet, but he effortlessly moved her.

"This is police brutality! Who do you think you are? I am not the criminal, I am a victim here! I want to see the girl cop; she was way nicer than you, Mack!"

He escorted her to his unmarked, dark-gray Chrysler and placed her in the back of the car. He walked to the driver's side, got in, and started the engine.

"You have the wrong person. I did not do this! She is my roommate. I am not a killer! You have to let me go!"

Agent Ryan ignored her, knowing there would be plenty of time to explain once he knew she was safe in custody. He kept an eye on Rachel as she sat in the back seat. Even though he had to keep his "cop face" plastered on his face, he felt sorry for her. She had no idea what she was in the middle of and the dangerous position she was in; she just didn't know. He was assigned to keep her alive and if that meant arresting her, so be it.

Rachel became unusually silent. She just wanted to curl up in a corner and block everything out of her mind. If she knew how bad this day was going to end up, she would have stayed in bed.

The FBI building located in downtown Harrisburg looked like any other government building. Large glass windows, surrounded by concrete. The looming concrete eagle on the front of the building looked more like a planter to Rachel than a significant symbol of the bureau. The inside of the building was lacking color and style.

The ape of a man, Ryan, practically dragged her out of his car. She almost stumbled trying to keep up with his pace when he managed to get her into the building.

Gordon placed her in an interrogation room before spying the infuriated glare of his boss's face. The commander pointed at his office door and quickly entered. He waited less than three seconds before he bellowed for Gordon to join him. "Ryan! In my office. Now!"

Gordon hurried to join his commander and face his wrath. "Sir, I just got back."

"Do you have any idea how important it is to get that information from her?"

"Yes, sir," Gordon answered his commanding officer, Albert Anderson.

"I told you to keep her safe and find out what she knows. You were supposed to approach this gently, gain her trust, and get her to reveal what she knows. She's very important to our case!"

"Yes, sir, I..."

Anderson cut him off before he could get all of his answer out. "You bring her in here crying and in handcuffs? Christ, Ryan, the girl just saw her roommate's dead body. And we don't know if she knows about Mrs. Harrison, do we?"

"No sir, "

"We have seasoned officers that cannot handle the scene that she saw in that bedroom. How many times do I have to tell you to show compassion?"

"I'll fix it. I'll make it right with her and get the information." Gordon tried to reassure him.

"You'd better. Your ass is on the line here. And my ass is hanging out there as well. We have opened this investigation and we cannot fail. Don't fuck this up!"

"I won't, sir, I'll keep her safe and get the information. After all, how could she resist my charms?" Gordon tried to lighten the mood of his superior.

"Get the fuck out of here and don't blow this," Anderson yelled.

Anderson sat at his desk and popped a few antacids. He knew that he picked his best agent to handle the matter. And from the looks of the beautiful Rachel Perry, Gordon would have his hands full. She looked like a spitfire.

Rachel sat on a cold-metal chair, in a chilly, block-walled room. They placed her at a table with two chairs on the opposite side of the metal table and another chair next to her. The handcuffs were moved so that her hands were in front of her instead of behind her back, but she was still in cuffs. And the agent had restrained her in front of the entire neighborhood. She was finished crying and growing angrier with each passing moment she had to sit in the freezing in the room.

She watched enough Law and Order to know how this was going to go down. They would drill her for hours, trying to wear her down and into a confession. That's what happened on all the cop shows. And the freeze-out was just another interrogation room tactic to get people to talk. *They're probably already looking at me through the two-way mirror*, she thought as she caught a glimpse of herself in the glass. Rachel could not remember a time when she looked so disheveled. She looked positively medieval. Her hair looked like she got caught in a tornado. Her raccoon eyes made her look crazy. If eyes were the windows of the soul, she thought they'd lock her up for sure. *This is why people always have crazy eyes in mug shots.*

If Rachel did not despise her father, she would have called him and asked him to represent her. Pride won out over common sense, so she did not ask to make her one call. That's what you do on every show; you lawyer up.

Rachel saw the metal door open and the obnoxious Agent Ryan entered the room. She held her handcuffed arms close to her chest and had a hard time containing her anger.

"Miss Perry, what I did was necessary to keep you safe." He did not see the point of not getting straight to it.

"You handcuffed me and threw me in the back of your police car. Oh, and in front of all my neighbors! Let's not forget that part! Are you going to tell me that was for my own good? My neighbors saw that! My landlord saw you arrest me after I found my roommate dead in my apartment. What the heck do you think they are all thinking?" She slammed her handcuffed wrists onto the table. "Ouch, Christ that hurt," she rubbed at her wrists.

Gordon tried to remain calm. He took a deep breath before answering her and her glowing green eyes. Her fiery hair seemed to have deepened with her temper. "Yes, that was unfortunate, but as I said, it was for your own good."

"How exactly is this for my own good? And why am I still handcuffed? I need these hands; I am a hairstylist. Do you think I'm planning an escape or something?" She shook her arms at him in fury.

"No, of course not," he answered as he removed the cuffs. His face was emotionless, but he felt his patience wearing thin.

Rachel began rubbing at her reddened wrists. "I know my rights. I want a lawyer," she fumed.

"You don't need an attorney. I am not charging you with any crime, Miss Perry," he said, realizing that he handled this whole situation extremely badly. It was another reason to blame Michelle. Having to deal with her made him as angry as a bull.

Gordon had no idea how he was going to get her to trust him and give him the information that he needed. His job depended on it. Her life depended on it.

"Then you have to let me go. I want to go home," she said, rising from her chair. "Well maybe not home, but to Valerie's apartment. I can stay there and sort this out. I'll move in with her. I doubt I'll get my security deposit back," she rambled. "I just need to get my things out of the apartment."

"Right now you can't. Your apartment is a crime scene and you can't go near anyone else, don't forget that."

"What? How could I forget? How will I *ever* forget? *My room-mate was murdered.* I saw her. I *saw* what they did to her." Panic and grief began to make Rachel's chest hurt. She stood and began to pace around the room. "And what do you mean I can't see anyone? Val is my best friend. I have to see her and I have to go to work; not to mention Dolores and Angela's funerals. I never thought I would have to say that. My friends are dead. One has a car accident and one was killed by a break in."

"Rachel, uh Miss Perry, please sit down. I need to talk to you about this."

"I don't know anything. I already told you."

"We believe that Miss Wright was not the target of this killer. We believe it was not a random break in."

"What's this *we believe* crap? Well, of course it was. Didn't you see what they did to the apartment? I know it was not an accident what they did to her. They shot her in the head. That was no accident. Maybe she startled them as they were looking for whatever they were trying to steal. She gets a little crazy over everything being in its place. So maybe she started freaking out about the mess they were making or something and they shot her. But that doesn't explain why she was in bed. You don't think she had a lover, do you? Maybe someone I don't know about did this. Maybe he went nuts and trashed the place. She could drive anyone crazy."

"No, Miss Perry. We believe that it was intended for you," Gordon said bluntly.

"*Me? Why me?* I've never hurt anyone," she said, trying to think of who would want to kill her. Her mind went immediately to the other night at the bar. Richard screamed that he would kill her after she kneed him in the nuts.

"If this has to do with Richard, I'll do more than knee him in the balls. No. That stupid man can barely tie his own shoes. There's no way he killed someone," Rachel answered with confidence.

"No, Miss Perry, this has to do with Dolores Harrison."

"Call me Rachel, alright? What are you saying? Why does anyone think this is related to Dolores? They barely knew each other." Rachel became more agitated. Tears filled her eyes again as she flopped into a chair.

"Mrs. Harrison didn't die from that auto accident. She was shot."

"*Shot?* No, the reporter said it was an *accident*, I heard it. Anyway, who would do that to her? Dolores was a wonderful, caring person. Who would want her dead?"

"Who indeed?" questioned Gordon.

"And you think I know the answer to that?"

"We believe that someone thinks you know a lot about Mrs. Harrison."

"Here we go again with the *we believe*. Of course, I know a lot about her. She's been my client and my friend for years," Rachel said proudly. "She was like a second mother to me. I loved her," Rachel's voice began to crack.

"Exactly," he responded. "So, until we catch the perpetrator, I'm afraid you are stuck with me."

"Uh, guess again, buddy," Rachel countered with a renewed hatred for the guy. "I'll take my chances with the crazy killer before I'm strapped to you for any amount of time. You're intolerable," Rachel alleged as she grabbed for her purse and her cell phone that were sitting on the chair next to her.

Gordon grabbed her phone from her. She tried to get it from him, but he was too tall for her to reach when he held it over his head.

"Hey, give me back my phone! I have to call Val. She'll be worried about me," she whined.

"Not on this phone, it's probably being monitored," he simply stated.

"Right, monitored, huh," she said. "Okay, Mr. Paranoid, just give me back my phone and let me go."

"Not a chance, Miss Perry."

"Trust me; I'll make your life hell if you don't." From the look on her face, Gordon knew she meant it.

"Oh, sweetheart you have no idea how much trouble I can make for you," he said losing his temper just as the chief entered the room.

"Ryan! Get her out of here and somewhere safe. Take her into hiding until we can figure out what to do with her," Anderson barked.

"Are you in charge around here?" Rachel planted her hands on her hips. .

"I am."

"Okay, tell this six-foot gorilla to give me back my phone and let me go," she said, jumping and trying to retrieve her phone again.

"Miss Perry, you are either going to cooperate with Agent Ryan or spend some time in a nice cell. Do I make myself clear?"

Rachel felt the wind being knocked out of her sails. The commander was not in the mood for her antics.

"Perfectly," she snipped as she stopped jumping and folded her arms on her chest.

Agent Ryan gave her a smug look that said *I have won*. Rachel continued to pout, not liking ever losing to any man.

The commander was not finished.

"Agent Ryan, get control of this situation or I'll bury your useless ass in paperwork for the next twenty years, got it?"

"Yes, sir," Gordon dropped his arms.

Rachel grabbed her phone.

Gordon grabbed it again and without much effort, broke it in two.

Commander Anderson suddenly needed more antacids and retreated to his office without another word.

CHAPTER
SIX

"You idiot! Your man killed the wrong girl," the caller exclaimed.

"Yes, it was an honest mistake," Eric declared without emotion. He was used to killing, not giving the order to kill. Eric attributed his unique talent for murder without feelings to watching his father beating his mother every time he got drunk. The last time was too much for Eric and, at seventeen, he committed his first murder when he took a baseball bat to his inebriated father's skull. Right there in the kitchen, he slugged him and watched him pitch forward, falling face first in front of his mother and foster sister. His father was too drunk and exhausted from beating on his wife to realize he had been hit.

Eric was tried and convicted as a juvenile and served ten years until his shady lawyer got him off on a technicality.

His mother passed away from cancer while he was serving time. She'd never visited him or thanked him for saving her from her abuser. She blamed him until her dying breath for taking away the one man that she ever loved. So, Eric wrote her memory off and moved on. The wall against emotion had been built.

His foster sister visited him often and they became very close. Closer than he ever thought he could be with anyone. They shared secrets.

She got mixed up with the wrong people when she was young, but he could tell that she was trying to straighten herself out. She even got a job and talked about moving up in the world, no matter what it took.

Eric found out in prison that he had a knack for finding people like himself; lost souls that had so much anger that the only thing that would quench it would be to hurt someone else. A kind of transference of pain. Maybe the need to hurt people was genetic, he reasoned. His father did it. Apparently, his mother liked it. She never fought back, anyway. So genetically, he was destined to be either a sender or receiver of pain. He chose sender.

In prison, Eric would train the lost ones, the ones not strong enough to lead others. He gave them what they needed to make them do what he needed them to do. A Charlie Manson of sorts, only not that popular.

After he'd served his time, he made a small fortune with his man-for-hire business. More than he could snort up his nose or spend on prostitutes and expensive cars.

Eric's success depended on the people he hired to do the jobs and this job was big. He could not afford to have his guy mess things up. The rich people that were paying him demanded quick results and accuracy. So far, his man wasn't delivering. If he didn't stop messing up and drawing attention to himself, Eric knew that he would have to eliminate one of his best guys. His type of elimination was of the permanent kind. The kind where you fall asleep and never wake up.

His client was ripping him a new one and that only made Eric more irritated.

"That mistake can cost me everything. I hired you to be discreet and to do a job. I am throwing a lot of money your way to finish the job, so do it. Find it!" The caller hung up.

Eric dialed his man. As usual, he didn't pick up, which only infuriated Eric more. "You know I hate leaving messages, but in your case, I'm going to do it. Get the fuck off your lazy ass and finish this job! Get what I need, do the job and lose the FBI. If you cannot do this job, you'll find yourself unemployed. And I am sure you already know how I fire people, shit-for-brains!"

Ridge put out his cigarette and took another shot of Jack Daniels.

Chapter SIX

It helped calm him. He listened to the message from Eric and decided that when he was done he would be going on his own—after he planted a bullet into the brain of that son-of-a-bitch. Leaving him messages like that, calling him shit-for-brains, he had no clue exactly how far Ridge would go to be the best and not take orders from a has-been junkie.

He'd met Eric in prison and after he got out, it made sense to work with him and get some quick cash in his pocket.

Ridge looked around his surroundings and sighed. He hated living out of a hotel, but this one was a swank room. He knew the police would be combing through the apartment of that chick he enjoyed shooting. They would try to find any clues, so he needed to be sure that if they did find any traces of him, they would not be able to locate him. He had to become invisible; a ghost.

But they would not find any DNA from him. Ridge was sure of that. He was a professional and never left a trail to be followed. Never an address, a traceable phone or credit cards that could lead back to him. In fact, even his name was a fake. He truly was the Invisible Man.

A moment of doubt dared to enter his thoughts. Maybe he was slipping. He did mess up by killing the wrong girl and that had a huge impact on his confidence. The mayor's wife was easy. That took no effort at all. He didn't know why he assumed that the girl in that bed was the right target. He rushed and it cost him. He had an important and lucrative job to do and did not want to lose his status with Eric until he was ready to go out on his own. He took great pride in his work. He just got sloppy. It was easier to blame it on the bad pot he purchased on the street corner down from his hotel room. That was a much easier pill to swallow than admitting that he had made a mistake.

Sure, most people would not think killing people was a job, but it was. It paid really well. He lit another cigarette and finished off the bottle of Jack. The last thing he planned on doing was to call Eric when he finished the job. Then, when he got his money, he would kill him too.

CHAPTER SEVEN

Rachel was silent in the passenger seat of Gordon's car. The heaviness of grief and the infuriating anger that boiled inside her both mixed with the images of the stark-red blood that splattered Angela's room. She knew she would never forget the acrid scent of death. Her senses were so heightened, she could swear she smelled it in the air.

The sight of Valerie's apartment made Rachel visibly relax. Normalcy and Valerie's energy would make her feel better. "It's right here. That's it, pull over," Rachel said, pointing at the apartment building.

Rachel opened the car door the second Gordon threw it in park. She closed the door with a slam. She ran up the stairs to Valerie's apartment building. Gordon was only a few steps behind her.

Rachel rang the doorbell and desperately knocked.

"It's me, open up!" she shouted.

Valerie opened the door and flew into Rachel's arms.

"I've been worried sick about you. You did not answer your phone. I saw the news! Angela was on the news! What the hell's going on?" Valerie pulled Rachel into her apartment.

It did not take Valerie but a second to notice the tall, gorgeous man next to her friend. The overly serious scowl on his face did not deter from his attractiveness.

"Who's he?" Valerie said, letting go of Rachel to turn her attention to Gordon.

"This is Agent Ryan. FBI. He's apparently assigned to me or something. Val, he put me in handcuffs!"

"What? Valerie glowered at Gordon. "She's a hairstylist. You don't mess with her hands; that's how she makes a living."

Gordon could feel the tension headache crawling up his neck and resting between his eyes. He wondered how much money he had in his 401(k) and savings. Maybe it was the time to take an early retirement and dump Miss Perry off to his boss.

Rachel's shrill made the pounding in his head much worse.

"That's what I told him," Rachel added. "It's one thing to shackle someone's feet together. But it's another to bind the hands."

"It's disgusting," Valerie said.

"Val, he owes me a new phone. He broke mine," Rachel said with an annoyed tone.

"Wait, let's back up. He's assigned to you? Is that what you said? What is that about? What did you do?" Valerie questioned. "You were with me. I'll swear on a stack of Bibles." Valerie made a quick sign of the cross.

"The FBI—Agent Ryan here and his boss—thinks I'm the one they were after. They think Angela was a mistake. Val, they think someone wants me dead. And Val, they said Dolores was shot too. This is insane! When I got to the apartment it was trashed. Blood everywhere…"

Gordon interrupted. "Miss Perry, it would be better if you did not discuss this with anyone. Get your things so that we can go," he ordered.

"Bossy, isn't he? Cute, but bossy," Valerie observed.

"Hey, Ryan, back off. She's my best friend and I'll tell her whatever I want." Rachel's annoyance with Gordon was growing.

"You will put your friend's life in jeopardy. The less anyone knows, the better this will be for you and everyone you know." He turned his attention to Valerie. "And if you want to keep your best friend here safe, you'll not repeat any of this to anyone," he sternly stated. "And I mean *anyone*. Not your mother, your priest, not even your dog."

"Don't worry, Val. I'll see you on Tuesday at work," Rachel reassured her friend.

"That will not be possible," stated Gordon.

"Uh, yes I will. I work on commission, and that means I have to work or I'm not paid. I do not get vacation time or sick time, or FMLA. I'm going to work, period, end of discussion," Rachel said as she moved around Val's apartment. She gathered some of the things she kept there and borrowed other items from her friend. She was grateful she and Valerie shared their makeup and some of their clothing. Like sisters, she supposed. She was lucky since she was unable to enter her own apartment. *You can't cross an active crime scene.* Rachel wasn't sure if she ever wanted to step foot in that apartment again.

"Miss Perry, there will be no more talk of returning to work. You would be putting yourself at risk and then I wouldn't be doing my job keeping you safe, now would I?" Gordon reasoned.

"I don't give a damn about your job, Agent. I only care about keeping mine. You can either follow me to the salon or head your pompous butt back to Harrisburg, got it?" Rachel stood in front of Gordon, shoving clothes into a backpack that she borrowed from Valerie.

"We have to leave. Are you finished packing?" Gordon grew impatient.

She went to the bathroom and scooped up some hair products and her spare toothbrush.

"Yeah, I'm ready," she said, hugging her friend. "See you soon. Tuesday," she whispered in Valerie's ear.

Gordon drove to a hotel near Lancaster City Square. The newly renovated hotel was a great place to hide out for a few days and had been approved by Anderson. They were only blocks from the police station and could easily get out of the hotel or out of town if they needed to run. His phone continuously rang and he mumbled to himself when he checked his texts and voicemail.

Rachel guessed it was either that female cop or his boss who was about to boil Gordon's balls for screwing things up with her. Either way, he was not happy about the calls or texts and he was not answering them. His phone buzzed again when the caller left another message.

Gordon's face was stone hard and focused as they entered the hotel. He registered them under a fake name and paid cash for the room. Both keys were in his possession. There was no way in hell he was going to give her a key so that she could sneak in and out.

They entered the elevator and he pushed the button for the sixth floor. Threw a maze of turns, they found their room. Gordon opened the door, walked to the bedroom and placed his duffel bag on the bed. It was always ready for this type of emergency and contained all of his necessities, neatly folded and assigned.

He glanced over at Rachel who was pulling unfolded clothing out of her backpack. She sorted through the pile, found a sweater and dumped the rest of the pile on top of Gordon's duffel bag.

Gordon chose to ignore it and hold on to what little sanity he had left.

"Get comfy, Miss Perry. You are going to be here for a little while. At least until we can figure this out," Gordon said.

"Great, my dreams are coming true." Her sarcasm dripped from her words. "I finally found the man of my dreams and he handcuffs me and takes me to a swank hotel. My mother would be so proud."

Gordon decided not to answer her with his own sarcastic thoughts. His mind told him to stay as far away from her as he could. His body was having a different reaction. It was a shame she was so beautiful. The thought didn't make any sense. It was true she grated on every nerve in his body. Still, she was his type. She was medium height, had curves in all the right places and that mane of fiery hair matched her temperament—a slow burning fuse that ignited into an inferno. He couldn't help but notice the freckles across her nose and cheeks that drove him to distraction.

Gordon looked over at Rachel. She was abnormally silent as she sat upright on the bed, propped up with pillows and with her legs extended as she changed channels every few seconds.

There was nothing interesting on the television. Law and Order was out of the question. Click…so was Bones. Click…and NCIS. Click, click, and more clicks.

"Nothing but cop shows, it figures. I cannot stand this. I should be doing something," she sighed and began to inspect the ends of her hair for split ends.

"There's plenty to do here. We could go down to the gym and work out, we could swim."

"I should be doing something to help figure out what's going on with all these deaths. You said I was the reason. That is not sitting very well with me. I should be helping to find the person responsible or something."

"Just leave the detective work to the detectives," Gordon stated as he checked his phone for another text message from Michelle. "Christ, leave me alone, woman," he muttered. He returned his attention back to Rachel. "It's Saturday night. Let's go out. There's a great bar close by. We could walk there. What about that?"

"I don't think so."

"Why not?" Rachel's pouting was beginning to annoy him. "Rachel, please take this seriously. Someone wants to kill you. They want you dead. As soon as we figure out why and catch this guy, you can be free of me."

"That's tempting, Ryan, but I have no idea why anyone would want to kill me. I am taking this seriously. You won't let me help."

"We believe it has something to do with your connection to Dolores Harrison. Did she tell you anything? Someone trashed your apartment looking for something. Any idea what it might be?" Gordon questioned, pulling out a small tablet and pen.

"Like what?" Rachel frowned. She was not in the mood for an impromptu interview. "She told me lots of stuff. We confided in each other all the time. Have you ever heard about stylist/client confidentiality? What is said in the salon stays in the salon," Rachel said, as she perused the room service menu. "Want some mozzarella sticks and wings?"

"Please take this seriously, Rachel, and help me get this guy so that I..."

"So that you what? You can get rid of me? Oh, trust me, I want that more than anyone does, but I cannot help you. I still do not believe anyone is out to get me. I'm only here because your boss threatened to put me in jail."

"And he's serious. As he sees it, you're withholding information in an ongoing investigation. How about contributing to the crime?"

"Are you serious?" Rachel was pissed. "I would never do anything to hurt Dolores or Angela. You have no idea how losing them affects me. Dolores was like a second mother to me in many ways. How dare you even think I would want anything to do with her death or Angela's! Sure, she was a nightmare, pain in the ass roommate, but she always paid her share, kept the place spotless, and meant well!"

Gordon sighed and slowly shook his head. He put his hands up in front of himself. "Calm down, calm down. No one thinks you actually had anything to do with killing Mrs. Harrison or Miss Wright. We think Mrs. Harrison shared something with you and that information puts you in terrible danger. Someone is so threatened by this information that they would kill the mayor's wife."

Gordon stood and walked over to Rachel. He sat down to face her. He could see the pain in her eyes with the mention of Dolores' death. He wanted very much to console her, but he knew that would be crossing a professional line. She was such a tempting creature.

Rachel used the back of her hand to wipe away a stray tear and tried to focus on the television. She just wanted a few moments to get her emotions in check. She flipped the channel to the news. The news reporter was reporting on Dolores' death again. The news reporter was dressed in a sharp black dress with a form-fitting blazer. Rachel took note that the woman on the screen showed little to no emotion as she talked about her beloved friend. *Just doing her job*, Rachel thought to herself. Her report was vague and borderline monotone.

"The memorial service will be held on Monday at the Miller Funeral Home on Front Street in Harrisburg. There will be a private church service following the memorial service."

The screen moved to a picture of Oliver Harrison and his son, Nick, leaving their home. Rachel's eyes locked on Nick Harrison. He looked older, but just as handsome.

Gordon did not miss a trick. He suddenly knew why Dolores and Rachel were so close. There was a history there, more than just a client and hairstylist. He could see the way Rachel was staring at the picture of Nicholas Harrison. They had a past.

Rachel realized that she was taking an excessive amount of time looking at her past flame. She looked away and gave her attention back to the pain-in-her-ass, FBI Agent. "I am going there on Monday. I know that Val will want to go with me."

"You think your friend will keep you safe? This is not a game, Rachel. Don't think for a moment that someone won't use her to get to you." Gordon said as he stood and moved about the room. "And they might even expect you to show up at Mrs. Harrison's funeral." He went to the windows to scan the outside.

Rachel sighed. "Must you do that?"

"Do what?" he asked as he pulled the curtains closer together.

"Look out there like you're expecting something bad to happen at any minute. Sit down and relax. I cannot take your pacing around this room. I already feel like a caged animal and it has only been a few minutes. Let's order some bar food, hit the mini-bar and watch a movie, all right? I need a strong drink. I cannot even deal with all of this. I need a distraction."

"Fine," he said as he sat on the other bed, needing to keep some distance between them.

Rachel called the room service number, placed a sizable order, and hit the mini-bar. As long as the FBI was paying to keep her, she was going to pettishly annoy them by spending their money.

Thirty minutes later, Rachel was stuffing herself with potato skins, mozzarella sticks, nachos, and rum. Gordon ate some cheeseburger sliders and drank bottled water. His phone began to ring again and he ignored it.

Rachel decided to address the annoying and constant ringing. "Aren't you going to get that? What if it's important?"

Gordon ignored the query. "Do you always eat like that?" he questioned.

"Nice, change the subject. No, usually I follow it down with some Fudgy Pudgy ice cream. It's my favorite flavor. Why are you not answering that damn phone? Bet it's your girlfriend checking in on you. Are you going to tell her you're shacking up in a hotel room with another woman? You got a girlfriend, right?"

"Fudgy Pudgy?" I'm sure it does what the name implies. Although in your case, you must have a very high metabolism. You're not exactly gaining weight from your eating habits."

"Thanks, I think. You are avoiding my girlfriend question," she answered, frowning and switching the station to a movie channel. They were playing one of her favorite movies, *Come Back to Me*.

"Oh, good, it just started," she said, propping the pillows behind her and continuing to eat, leaving nacho crumbs on the bed.

Gordon rolled his eyes as he checked his phone messages.

Rachel glanced at him as he dialed a number from memory. He removed his jacket, tie, and dress shirt. Rachel could not remember a time when a man looked so damn sexy in a plain Fruit of the Loom under-shirt. It fit him like a glove; snug over his broad chest and sculpted upper arms. She watched as his face hardened when he began to speak.

"What do you want, Mickey? Gordon's voice hardened. His piercing eyes narrowed, rigid, hard. His free hand was fisted. His voice and remarks were clipped.

"We settled this. No, you don't need to know where we are. Oh, it's over, trust me."

Gordon ended the call without a good bye and lay back on his bed. He closed his eyes trying to get his ex out of his mind. Michelle Kinsley knew exactly how to get under his skin. There was a time when she was his whole world. He had wanted to marry her and start a family. But she decided to cheat with his best friend, Gary. He lost the two most important people in his work and in his life when he found out the truth. He would never get past her sleeping with his ex-best friend. He did not need either one of them. The entire affair taught him a valuable lesson—you can't trust anyone.

Rachel stopped chewing long enough to address his sour mood. "Was that your girlfriend?"

"She's not my girlfriend and this is not a conversation that we are going to have."

"Well, she was your girlfriend and by the look on your face, you still have feelings for her."

Gordon gave her a surprised look. He must be losing his touch if she could read his facial expressions enough to know that Michelle was anything more than someone that he did not like.

"Miss Perry, personal conversations are not appropriate. My job is to protect you and figure out who wants to harm you."

"Hmmm. That's a nice speech but she wants to see you very bad-ly. Maybe she isn't done with your relationship."

Gordon closed his eyes and decided the only way to get her to stop asking questions was to ignore her. He was tired and stressed. He pon-dered if there was a woman alive who did not ask questions and always wanted to talk about feelings 24-hours a day, 7-days a week.

Rachel waited until she heard his breathing become deeper and his eyelids move as though in a deep sleep. She carefully got off her bed so as to not disturb him and reached for one of the keys on the bedside table. As quick as a snake strike, he grabbed her arm, threw her onto his bed, and sat on top of her.

Rachel was face down in the pillow.

"Get off me, you big oaf!" she yelled. "You're blocking my ability to breathe, asshole!" she gasped.

He slightly lifted his body to give her a little more breathing room. In one swift movement, he flipped her over and handcuffed her to himself.

"Wait, what are you doing?" she huffed.

"I'm making sure you don't try anything stupid tonight. You're going to have to spend the night handcuffed to me."

"Are you kidding? That is police brutality. Let me go! You can't do this," Rachel cried.

"I just did. Didn't your parents ever teach you common sense?" He ripped the phone line out of the wall.

Rachel let out a stream of cuss words that would have made her grandmother smile and her mother faint. She pushed against his chest, trying to knock him off of her.

"Not a chance, princess. Until you start to take this seriously, I'm just going to have to keep you nice and close."

"Let me go, you pervert. I'll scream and then they'll be people running in here. What's your cop girlfriend going to say about the fact that you're are handcuffing yourself to other women? Bet that will piss her off."

Rachel could tell by the look on his face that she hit a nerve. His guard was down just long enough to validate what she had already known. There was history between them. Maybe something unresolved.

Gordon was struggling to gain composure. "Scream and you'll be sucking on my sock," he threatened. The look on his face told Rachel that he was serious. He was just mean enough to stuff his worn sock into her mouth; there was no doubt about it. Rachel stopped squirming.

Gordon lifted himself off of her and sat next to her on the bed. "The only time I will uncuff you tonight is to use the bathroom. The rest of the time, I'm afraid you'll be right here."

"Hey, I don't share beds with total strangers."

"Believe me, Rachel, that is the very last thing on my mind."

It annoyed her the way he said it; as if sleeping with her would be disgusting or something.

"Hmm, well when you put it that way, how could I refuse?" she countered with a mood.

"You can't."

Rachel grew silent in the passing hours. The food and alcohol were making her sleepy. Usually Saturday night meant she did not go to bed until after 2 a.m. Yet, it was only 10 p.m. and she was exhausted. She chalked it up to the incredibly stressful day. Secretly, she was afraid to go to sleep and relive the images of blood spatter and Angela's brain splattered all over her white walls. That picture would forever be etched in her mind. The metallic smell of blood, the image of all that red in contrast to all that white. Rachel shook her head in an attempt to clear it. She decided to relax and deal with all of it in the morning.

The next thing she knew, she was awakened by a sound in the hallway. Her mind was still foggy with sleep and dreams of a sexual nature. She had a graphic image of Gordon Ryan passionately kissing her, running his hands down her body and, sweet Jesus, making her shudder with pleasure. She sighed at the warmth of a man tucked in tight behind her. He was spooning her. Her groggy mind was the reason she enjoyed the sensation when he shifted even closer.

The coldness of the metal handcuffs against her skin caught her attention. Her eyes flew open wide. It all rushed back. The murders, the vomiting on Gordon's shoes, the hotel, and the handcuffs. All of it, every gruesome detail consumed her mind until there was no room for anything else.

Gordon shifted. His handcuffed arm tried to pull her closer. Rachel thought he would be humiliated if he knew how he held her in the middle of the night. She had to admit it felt comforting safely wrapped in his arms. Rachel closed her eyes and her mind to the terror and allowed herself to enjoy the warmth of his body next to hers—just a little while longer.

CHAPTER EIGHT

The light coming in the window started to wake Gordon. As he breathed in, the smell of her hair filled all his senses. It took his brain several seconds to register just how amazingly perfect her body felt and how wrong it was to have her so close.

If she's awake, she's good at faking sleep, he thought as he tried to move away from her. He knew he needed to put some serious distance between their bodies immediately. Her warmth and softness and the scent of her was causing an unprofessional reaction in him. Damn she was warm and comforting. He had to move quickly. It had been a long time since he woke up next to a woman and his reaction was becoming painful.

He uncuffed himself and made his way to the bathroom, hoping he was done before she woke. He heard the television turn on and knew she was awake.

"Rachel?"

"Hmm."

"Go ahead and order some breakfast."

"I don't eat breakfast, just coffee," she answered.

"Well, I eat. Order something," he shouted from the bathroom.

"Say please," she answered loudly. She heard him swear and knew she was getting under his skin.

"Jesus, Rachel, do we have to start this already?"

"Didn't your mother ever teach you any manners? I don't take well to demands." She snickered to herself.

"Alright, could you please order something for breakfast?" He said it as sweetly as he could manage between his clenched teeth.

Gordon remembered waking up so close to her. He realized that he preferred her quiet and sleeping. That seemed the only time that she did not get on his last nerve.

"Yes, sweetheart, what would you like?" she asked as sweetly as possible.

"Pancakes and sausage would be great."

"Want juice?"

"Tomato."

"Yuck!" she said and made a face.

"Well, feel free to not order one for yourself," he answered bluntly and exited the bathroom.

She dialed the number and placed the order before turning her eyes to his. He was again dressed in a button-down shirt and black pants. She looked away and back to the television that was playing news about the death of Dolores Harrison, and now a new report about the murder of Angela. The reporter did not give out Angela's name, but they did show a picture of her apartment building. The image turned to a video of Gordon placing Rachel in the back of his unmarked car.

"There were reporters outside my building? They have me on film in handcuffs and you are throwing me in the back of your car!"

"I did not throw you, Rachel."

"Well you threw me under a bus! Now everyone who watches the news, and that's like everyone I know, will all think I killed her!" Rachel's hands fisted in her hair.

What would Shirley think? The thought of Shirley made her think of the salon and the Gossip Gal Gang. "They are going to rip me to shreds!"

"Who is going to rip you to shreds?"

"The gang! They never let anything go. When they find out, I might as well jump off the top of this hotel. My life will be over."

"Wait a minute." Gordon was confused. *If Rachel was messed up in some sort of gang, maybe that was the reason. It had to be,* he thought. "Who is this gang? Who is the leader?"

"Well, Shirley. She's the ringleader and everyone follows her lead. She's also my boss, so you see how this is going to be really bad."

"Let me get this straight. Your boss leads the gang."

"Yes, pay attention! They are going to find out and it's going to spread like herpes in a whorehouse. That's actually Valerie's saying. It's catchy."

"So your friend is also a member of this gang?"

"Oh, God no! But she is victimized by their brutality every now and again. We all are. Even when you don't know it. They're stabbing you in the back."

Gordon began to dial his phone and pace. "Chief, I got a lead. Can you find out what gangs there are in Lancaster?"

"What? Why in the world would you need his help? I know where they live." Rachel shook her head trying to reason why he was so worked up over a group of backstabbing, gossip-loving old biddies. "They live within two square blocks of the salon. What the hell do they have to do with this?"

Gordon looked at her as if she had just lost her mind. "It has everything to do with this. You should have told me sooner. Important information like this, Rachel, is exactly the thing you need to share."

He grabbed a pen out of the night stand and began to write on a napkin. "Thanks, Chief, I'll check in later. Let me get more information out of Miss Perry and I'll report this afternoon."

Gordon hung up and ran his fingers through his hair. He felt exasperated by Rachel and her lack of seriousness over the situation. His mind buzzed with possibilities and theories.

"Rachel, is this a large gang?"

"Well, it depends on the day, but who cares about that right now?"

"I do. How many members do you think there are?" Gordon took a sip of water.

"Well if you count the new people that just started coming, I would say about two hundred and fifty."

Gordon choked on his water. "Two hundred!"

"And fifty. That might be a little low, actually. Shirley had been using the newspaper ad to bring in more people."

"She put an ad in the paper?"

"What's wrong with you? Of course she put an ad in the paper, how else do you draw in more people? You have to advertise if you want to get more, that's how business works."

Rachel was tired of the conversation about the gang. She knew that it was only a matter of time until her parents would realize that she was missing and would start to worry. Well, her mother would, anyway.

"I need to call my parents. My mom will be worried, especially since I'm not answering my phone. By the way, you need to replace that today. I need a phone."

"I agree with you contacting your parents, but you cannot tell them what's going on. You will only put them in danger as well. The less people involved, the better, remember? We'll go to the library and you can email them, how does that sound?"

"It sounds stupid. The library is not open until tomorrow. I need to call them today."

"Alright, alright, why don't we stop in? Do they live close by? I'll send a few police officers to patrol the neighborhood before we go and make sure that nothing looks suspicious," he said, judging her reaction with confusion. He sensed a hesitation.

"You want to go with me to meet my parents?" Her hands flew in the air. "Are you kidding me? You cannot go! Oh, yeah, I can see that conversation. Hi Mom, hi Dad, I would like you to meet my FBI handler. He's investigating the murder of my friends and trying to keep me safe. I slept in the same bed with him last night because he handcuffed me to himself. How are both of you? How's Grandma?" she said sarcastically.

"We'll just have to lie. Tell them I'm your new boyfriend or something. I'm sure they're used to those kinds of visits."

"Why do you say that?" Her shackles were up. Thinking of shackles she raised her arm. "Are you ever going to remove the handcuffs?"

"Yes, sorry." He reached into his pants pocket and found the key. He unlocked the cuff and removed it from her arm. "I just meant that you being you, uh, you probably don't have any problem getting guys to fall for you."

"You assume a lot." Her thoughts went to her recent date with the Dickster. "The only time men fall for me is when I knee them in the balls. It's sad, but true," she answered.

The conversation dropped as someone knocked on the door and identified himself as room service. Rachel approached the door, but Gordon pushed her back, pulled out his gun and looked through the peephole. He opened the door slowly.

Instead of letting the person wheel the cart into the room, he took the cart, tipped the man, and wheeled it in himself. Gordon placed the cart at the end of his bed and took a seat. He removed the silver tray cover and began to dig in.

Rachel silently sipped on her coffee and watched the television.

"What's wrong with you?" Gordon asked. You're suddenly unusually quiet."

"Nothing. Everything."

He stopped eating and looked over at her. "Rachel, what's wrong? I mean, I know what's wrong. You've been dealt a real bad hand."

"I don't know, just calculating up all the crap from the last few days. I lost someone very important to me, my roommate was killed, I'm stuck here with you, and you snore in your sleep! I have to face my father, and I don't have the energy for it all."

"Yes, I am aware of all of that. I know things are a mess for you right now, but you have to stay strong and pull yourself together. You have to listen to me so that I can keep you safe. That includes facing your family. You cannot let them know what's going on. You will put their lives in danger as well."

"I know that part. You wouldn't understand. You probably come from a very nice, loving family. That's not the way it is in my family."

"Problems with your parents?"

"Not parents, just one of them. Dad is the problem. Well, actually, I am the problem. He's disappointed in me. I went to Penn State for a few semesters and I left to go to cosmetology school. I hated the college scene. It just wasn't for me. He wanted me to be an attorney like him. He said I was too smart to throw my life away on a frivolous job, trying to make women love themselves. I had potential and I was better than the average person working a meaningless job. What's the difference? I provide a service to people and as an attorney, he does the same.

I called him a snob and we've had this thing between us ever since. I'm a big disappointment to him. And he's waiting for me to fail and come crawling back to him so that he can be right."

"Let me ask you something. Are you happy? Does your job make you happy?" Gordon placed his hands on his hips and stood over her

"Of course. I love what I do. Creativity and artistry. It's a lot of pressure. Women put so much stock in their appearance. Society makes them that way. I help them create the look that's right for them."

"You really are passionate about your work. Then screw him." Gordon smiled at her.

"Yeah, screw you, Daddy, I'm happy. That will go over really well. My mother would faint." Rachel smiled.

"Okay, maybe you don't say screw you to your father."

Rachel laughed and Gordon noticed that beautiful smile.

"My mother would shit a brick if I talked to him that way," she giggled.

"Well, I can't wait to meet them."

"Well, there's no time like the present. That is, if you think it's safe to go now." Her voice was quiet.

"We'll go in a little while. Let me finish eating, all right? I will contact the officers we have guarding their home and make sure there has been no activity." He could not help but smile at her. "Trust me, you will get through this."

"I am starting to. Trust you, that is." Rachel blushed and sent him a killer grin.

"Okay, that's progress." Gordon dug into his food. He was used to eating fast. It was a cop thing. You never knew when the next call would come, so you ate quickly.

"Alright," she smiled. She knew he was starting to loosen up. It was probably killing him to be so nice to her. He was good at the abrasive cop thing.

Rachel was better at reading people and she knew he had a soft side somewhere. Still, she felt like a trapped animal. Rachel was determined to be nice to Agent Ryan and cooperate. She could probably get more freedom and maybe even lose him if she cooperated. She wanted normalcy back. She wanted all of it to be over.

Deep down, Rachel knew he was just trying to do his job, which meant keeping her alive.

Oliver Harrison paced in the living room of Carla Cassidy's condo in Marietta. Carla was stretched out on the couch like a satisfied cat. "Oliver, will you stop pacing. You are making me dizzy."

"How am I supposed to be calm? The media is all over me right now. Look how I had to sneak around just to see you last night. Spending the night here was a mistake. I'm thankful that I wasn't followed and leaving here will be easier than leaving my home."

Carla's feelings were hurt. "I thought that now you would be free to come and go whenever you wanted. You are not married now."

"Jesus, Carla, my wife isn't even in the ground yet and you are thinking I should just be open about our affair? Don't be so naive. You've placed far too much importance on yourself."

"What are you saying? That if it wasn't me you've been screwing for the last six months, it would be someone else?"

"Everyone is replaceable. I think it's time for me to leave."

CHAPTER NINE

Valerie woke early for a Sunday morning. She had a lot on her mind, mostly Rachel's safety.

She dressed in her black yoga pants and a big sweatshirt. She did not intend to actually pop in a yoga DVD and exercise, she just liked the way the clothes felt.

Valerie hoped Rachel would find a way to contact her. Rachel had seen her through a lot in her life, including the drunk driving accident that killed both her parents and her brother. Rachel's friendship was the one solid thing in her life and if she lost her, she truly felt that she would die. Now, the FBI dude was another subject. He was hot, sexy and seemed to have his act together. He was perfect for Rachel, even if it seemed her friend could not stand him.

Valerie walked to her favorite café in hopes Rachel would show up. She sat for about an hour and sulked into her hot chocolate and bagel and egg sandwich. The stress of waiting for Rachel to contact her was playing on her. She was not even in the mood to flirt.

Valerie watched John Smith walk in and take a seat near the windows. He never even looked in her direction. And she was grateful since she wasn't exactly dressed for sexual success. It gave her a moment to study him without being noticed. My God, he was built like a muscled jock; his arms were solid without even flexing them. He dressed impeccably well. John Smith seemed to always dress in grays or blacks. With his expensive looking pants, black shoes and a grayish-black shirt, she could only describe his look as mysterious. Way out of her league, she determined with a shrug.

Valerie loved to watch people and she scanned the room. To John Smith's right, there was a couple in a heated argument, the next table was a man typing away on his laptop. A woman caught her attention. She too was scanning the room. Not in a casual way. It was an intense view of the people at every table and her eyes settled on Valerie.

Valerie gave her a small smile. The woman didn't reciprocate the gesture. She moved her gaze on to the other tables. Valerie ate her bagel and drank her drink. She continued to feel the woman's gaze return to her over and over again. Valerie could see her out of the corner of her eye watching her. She casually stood and threw away her trash, put on her coat and decided she had had enough of the staring woman—it was time to leave.

She noticed John Smith had already left the cafe.

Valerie walked to the little store on the corner to pick up a few groceries and to say hello to Sal, the owner.

When Valerie came out of Sal's she saw the woman again. They made brief eye contact before the woman got into a gray sedan.

Valerie walked quickly back to her apartment and bolted the door. *These murders are making me paranoid,* she thought before checking the lock a few more times.

"I shouldn't talk ill of the dead." She made the sign of the cross. "But dammit, now I'm starting to act as crazy and paranoid as Angela."

CHAPTER TEN

"Right here on the left," Rachel said, pointing at her parent's home.

The stone house located outside of Lancaster city, was beautiful, roomy, and elegant. Gordon pulled up to the huge wooden door. A slight elderly woman opened the front door and walked down the front porch stairs and to Gordon's car. She opened Rachel's door before Gordon had a chance to get out of the car.

"Oh, my girl! I saw the news! Are you alright? Where have you been?" Maria hugged Rachel as she exited the car.

"Hi, Maria, I should have called," Rachel said, hugging the elderly woman.

"Your mother is beside herself. She tried to call you several times. Come in and I'll put some tea on," Maria said. Gordon caught her attention. "And who is this handsome stranger?"

Rachel cleared her throat nervously. "Um, Maria, this is Ryan, uh… Gordon Ryan. He's my, uh, friend."

Gordon came to stand beside Rachel and placed his hand on the small of her back. The gesture of intimacy made Rachel tense.

Gordon's handsome smile made Maria blush. "Hello. Maria, is

it? My name is Gordon Ryan and I am Rachel's boyfriend." The lie spun off his tongue effortlessly.

"Well of course you are. I mean, you would have to be if Rachel is bringing you here. Come in, come in. She never brings her beaus here. Why, I do not think I have met anyone since Nick. How long has it been, Rachel, eight, nine years? Oh his poor mother, Dolores. She was such a nice lady."

"Yes she was wonderful," Rachel mumbled. "Gordon, Maria works for my parents. She helped to raise me," Rachel certainly did not want to discuss Nick Harrison or the death of Dolores. She walked in the front door and threw her backpack onto the floor.

Maria was still talking. She was never shy to offer her opinion or a comment.

"I saw you too. Your father was livid when he saw you on the news being handcuffed. Your mother cried and that's when she tried to call you several times. The call just kept going to your voicemail. Your parents will be down in a few minutes. Prepare yourself."

Maria disappeared into the kitchen, leaving Gordon and Rachel alone in the foyer. Rachel turned to Gordon with a warning look on her face.

"Okay, hot shot, no funny business," she warned.

"Just taking it all in." He gave her a half-hearted smile. "That Maria is a feisty woman."

A beautiful woman entered the foyer area. There was no mistaking that she was Rachel's mother. She had the same shade of red hair, slim-build and same eyes. It was obvious that Mrs. Perry took very good care of herself.

She rushed over to Rachel and hugged her. "I tried to call you. What happened Rachel, why were you arrested?" Margaret Perry eyed Gordon suspiciously. She was trying to determine where she had seen him before. "Well, Rachel, why are you standing here? Don't be rude, dear, I'm sure our guest would be more comfortable in the sitting room, don't you think?" Margaret Perry said as she kissed her daughter's cheek. She took a moment to admire the fine catch that her daughter brought home. His chiseled chin, broad shoulders and muscled arms certainly got a woman's attention, no matter what the age.

"Mom, we really can't stay too long. I just wanted to let you know that my phone had a little accident and I need to get a new one, so if you try to call me, I won't answer. I didn't want you to worry. Also, I didn't do anything wrong, I just had to go down to the police station to make a statement, that's all."

"In handcuffs? Well, I can see you are in some capable hands here," Margaret said as she made eye contact with Gordon. Gordon smiled and nodded his head.

"Really, Rachel, you were not raised by wolves. I surely hope that the time you spent in boarding school would have taught you better manners," Margaret scolded as she shifted her eyes from Rachel to Gordon.

"Oh! Mom, this is Gordon. Gordon, this is my mother, Margaret,"

Gordon put out his hand to shake Margaret's hand. She was left with an immediate impression.

"Strong, assertive and some kind of professional."

"You have no idea," muttered Rachel.

"Alright, come in, Gordon, may I take your coat," Margaret offered.

"Oh, really, as Rachel said, we can't stay too long."

"Is *he* here?" Rachel whispered.

"If you are referring to your father, yes he is. He is in his study. You should prepare yourself for his anger. You know how he gets when you embarrass him. Maybe you should go in and say hello and have a private conversation," Margaret said, hoping her two favorite people would put their silly hostility behind them.

"No, you know how that *always* ends up. He says something, I respond and the next thing you know, we're arguing again. I can't take it, Mom. Not today. You are just going to have to get used to the fact that Daddy and I don't see eye to eye on certain things," Rachel responded sharply.

At the sound of voices, Mitchell Perry exited his study to find his daughter and a tall gentleman standing in the foyer. "What did you do this time?" Mitchell scowled at Rachel as he joined the group.

"Ya see!" Rachel said to her mother. "I'm not in the house ten minutes and already he's insinuating that I'm in some kind of trouble."

Gordon sarcastically cleared his throat. It was a reminder to Rachel that she actually was in trouble; a whole mess of trouble, and that she had no idea how or why or what to do about it.

"Alright, got to go," Rachel said, turning toward the door.

"What? You have not been here in two months. Can't you at least spend a few minutes with your mother? Maybe you would like to explain why you were all over the news getting arrested?" asked Mitchell.

"Fine," Rachel said, stomping into the sitting room with everyone following behind her.

Maria appeared with a tray of crackers, cheese, chocolate chip cookies, and hot tea. "Rachel, how does your new boyfriend like his tea?" Maria questioned.

Rachel looked over at Gordon, who was sitting beside her on the couch. He merely lifted an eyebrow at her. He loved watching her struggle for answers, since she clearly knew nothing about his likes and dislikes. However, Rachel did not really care how he liked it.

"Lots and lots of sugar and extra cream," she answered, assuming he would take his black.

Let him choke on that, she thought.

"Touché," he whispered in her ear. Gordon raised his cup and took a sip. It was disgustingly sweet and with all the sugar and cream, it barely resembled tea. He managed a smile at Maria.

"It's perfect, Maria," he lied. "Just like I like it, sweet. Like our Rachel, here."

Maria's ego puffed up as evidenced by the huge smile on her face. She certainly saw what Rachel saw in the young man. Handsome, charming and pleasant. He had all the qualities of a fine husband.

Mitchell was eager to get the rundown on the man who apparently was spending time with his daughter. He hoped that she would settle down, get married, and maybe go back to college. Maybe put the silliness of playing hairdresser out of her head. She was brought up in the finest schools and had a chance at several great colleges. She could have married the mayor's son, but she blew that dream. That's the way he saw it. He knew he was not good at hiding his contention for her life choices. He knew he raised her better than hanging out in bars, running around with that loose Valerie girl and barely making enough money to support herself. It was very difficult for him not to try to convince her to make better choices. Success was measured in money. Therefore, Mitchell wanted to find out all that he could about the new man in her life and he was not going to waste any time. "So, Mr. Ryan, what do you do for a living?"

Before her father could get into drilling Gordon for information, Rachel interrupted. "Mom, Dad, I have something to tell you before we get into all of that."

Mitchell Perry pounced. "Dear God, she gets arrested *and she's* pregnant! I knew it! I knew it was just a matter of time before she got herself knocked up, with that alternative lifestyle of hers. Is he the father? Of course he is, why else would you bring him here, you never bring any of them here."

"Daddy, shut up!" Rachel yelled. "Christ, I am not pregnant! Right away, right away, you assume that I did something else to mess up my life. I've had it!"

Mitchell was stunned at the way Rachel addressed him. He was too shocked to respond.

Margaret was appalled at the choice words her daughter used to disrespect her father. "Young Lady, you apologize immediately to your father! Don't you dare come into the house and speak to your father like that!"

Rachel's eyes began to tear out of frustration, guilt, and loss. "What I was going to say is, I have to stay away for a while. Please don't ask me any questions, but know that I am alright."

Maria and Margaret gasped. Both women went to Rachel's side.

Mitchell shook his head. "And I suppose that is not suspicious at all. Telling us you have to stay away. Look how you have upset your mother!"

Gordon felt the need to step in. "Now, if we can all remain calm and talk about this. The yelling will get us nowhere."

"You see how he is! You see!" Rachel reached her limit and snapped. "All he cares about are appearances. He is so afraid that I'll shame him in some way, that he has no idea who the hell I am anymore," she said, close to tears. "And he doesn't care to find out. He just assumes and jumps to conclusions."

Mitchell felt guilty about doing just that, yet his pride demanded that he never admit when he was wrong. He was an attorney for goodness sake. They were never wrong. But she was right and that annoyed him.

Margaret was also tired of her husband's verbal stings where her daughter was concerned.

"Mitchell Perry, I thought I married a sensible, compassionate man. Stop acting like an ass," she shrieked.

"Margaret, dear, this is so unlike you; such language for an attorney's wife," Mitchell tried to diffuse the situation in his usual arrogant way.

"Don't you dare try to make this about me," Margaret scorned. "Don't you dare. Your daughter needs us; two people that she knew have died. Show some compassion." She looked at Rachel. "The news said Angela was killed? Killed how?"

Rachel finally decided she had had enough. She stood and grabbed her coat. "Gordon, let's go."

Margaret looked as if she was ready to kill her husband. "Oh, don't go, please, stay, Rachel. Stay for dinner, please," Margaret begged.

"No, Mom, I'm leaving. Until he changes, I'm not coming back," Rachel said as she stormed out of the sitting room and out the front door. Gordon was not far behind her.

"Rachel, I'm…"

"Don't say anything, just don't," she said with tears streaming down her cheeks.

Margaret finally realized where she had seen the man before. Her hand went to her heart. He was the man she saw on television who handcuffed Rachel and put her in the police car. She knew better than to tell her husband. What mess had her daughter become involved in?

Gordon checked his ringing phone and swore under his breath. "We got to go," he huffed as he shoved his phone back into its holder on his belt. He put his hand on the small of Rachel's back and guided her toward the door.

Rachel looked over her shoulder at her mother who was clearly upset and then to the stern stare of her father. He would never admit he was wrong. That would go against everything he ever knew about being an attorney. Never admit wrongdoing.

Rachel hung her head and let a hot tear slide down her cheek.

Gordon stood outside of his vehicle and kicked at his tire. "You ready to go? Hang on," he said as he grabbed his phone again.

Commander Anderson was on the line and did not sound very happy. "Ryan! You will be meeting with an agent from the Lancaster Humane League. Dolores Harrison's dog was taken there after her murder because no one in the family could handle this dog. There have been some issues with the animal at the Humane League as well. We do not want to put this dog down. It may have seen who killed Dolores. So congratulations, you are now the owner of a bitch."

"No way! That was not part of the deal! I'm not really the dog type and I already have my hands full here," he said as he regarded Rachel, who was picking at her nails and pacing outside of the car.

"You will do this and no complaints. This is the end of the conversation, Ryan. See if you can get the bitch to calm down. It bit two people so far at the Humane League." Anderson gave Gordon the meeting information and hung up before Gordon could protest again.

"Shit," he said under his breath. He looked over at Rachel who was eyeing him suspiciously. "Hey, Rachel, I have some news. We're going to have some company on this trip of ours."

"Who?"

"It's not a who; it's a what. Apparently, we now will have Dolores' dog tagging along with us."

"Muffin! Oh my God, I love that dog!" Rachel's face lit up for the first time.

"The dog that has bitten two people at the Humane League is called Muffin?"

"Well, yeah. Muffin is very selective as to who she likes. I never had any problems with her. I wonder why Oliver Harrison didn't take her. Never mind. I answered my own question. He's an asshole. That's why he didn't take her in."

"Yeah, I'm not really a dog person. How big is this dog anyway?" Gordon hated dogs ever since he had been bitten by the neighbor's dog when he was very small. He still had a slight scar on his chin from that mean St. Bernard named Sasha. That bitch was fierce! "So, tell me about this mutt we're now going to be stuck with."

Rachel could not resist lying to Gordon about Muffin, since he obviously hated dogs. "She's about one hundred pounds. I am not sure what kind she is. One of those Great Dane, Irish Wolfhound types. Tons of fur and hates men. That's probably why she attacked people. I bet you they were all men." She smirked.

"That's just fantastic." Gordon was not fearful of much in life. Nevertheless, the sound of this huge, man-hating fur ball sent a chill up his spine. "Any chance we get to lose this mutt?"

"Not on your life! Dolores loved that dog more than anyone did. We are not dumping her anywhere. Besides, you never know, she might be able to help."

"Well if we need help pulling a sleigh, I'll be sure to ask for her help."

They drove to the Lancaster Humane League in silence. Gordon was sulking over the unfavorable chain of events and Rachel was smiling to herself. She could not wait until Gordon actually saw Muffin's tiny stature. Make no mistake about it, Muffin was still a pint-sized handful, but seeing the big bad FBI agent, reacting to a dog with fear made her laugh. It made him human, full of emotions that sometimes he forgot he had.

"Maybe you should see this hairy creature first," Gordon said apprehensively as they pulled into the parking lot.

Rachel jumped out of the car and headed straight for the front door of the shelter. Gordon reluctantly followed.

Rachel addressed the clerk at the counter over the deafening sound of barking. It was endless and did nothing to improve the mood of Gordon. "Excuse me, I'm Rachel Perry, and this is Agent Ryan. We're here for Muffin."

"Oh, thank God!" The clerk practically jumped out of his chair.

Gordon stiffened. "It's really that bad?" Gordon grew pale.

The clerk nodded his head. "It's really that bad. Wait here and I'll get her." He disappeared behind a door and reappeared in less than five minutes. "She got me again, the little bitch!" Realizing what had slipped out of his mouth, he blushed. "Oh, sorry. But this dog is a menace."

"Muffin!" Rachel exclaimed. "You sweet little girl! Come to Rachel!" She put her arms out and Muffin began wagging her tail and kissing Rachel on the face.

Gordon backed away. "Ok, you got me. This pint-sized pooch can't be as bad as all that. Christ, she is licking you on the lips!"

"She is not. She's just a sweet little angel, aren't you, sweet baby. I had you worried, didn't I?" Rachel teased. "You should've seen your face!"

The clerk passed the paperwork over the counter to Gordon and then grabbed a paper towel to put pressure on the new bite mark that Muffin left as a parting gift. "I don't believe in euthanizing animals for the most part, but after a few days with this one, I could be persuaded to change my mind. Good luck," he scowled. "And good riddance," he said under his breath.

They drove only a few miles back to the hotel. As they entered the hotel, Rachel put Muffin into her oversized leopard-print purse. "Now you behave. Do not get us in trouble. I don't think we're supposed to have dogs in here."

Gordon scanned the lobby for anything out of order. There was a couple with a small child looking as though they were checking in at the front desk. A man with two teenagers was walking toward the front door and an elderly couple was standing near the elevator. Nothing gave off any signs of danger.

They took the stairs to the second floor and to their hotel room. Gordon used the key card and opened the door to their room. He was the first to notice the room was in shambles. He put an arm up to block her entrance. "We have to get back to the car," he demanded. "Go!"

She did not hesitate to follow his orders. They entered the elevator to be more visible to others and went to the lobby. Rachel did not look around. She just put her head down, walked to the parking garage and to his car, and sat in the front passenger's seat in shock.

He was talking to someone on the phone while he circled the car; checking underneath and under the hood before he slid into the driver's seat. She could hear him talking to someone about the hotel room and knew he was calling it in as a crime scene.

He got in the car and faced her. "I'm sorry, but we can't go back in and get your things. We'll get clothing later. I'll make sure that an officer gets your things after they investigate the room. Right now, we have to get out of here." He started the car and drove out of the city before either one said a word. Rachel sat peering out the window with Muffin curled up on her lap.

They drove on Route 30 for many miles. The scenery changed from city streets to farmhouses, barns, and Amish buggies.

Rachel wondered where they were going, but decided to keep silent. Neither one was in the mood to talk about what had just happened. She took stock of the past few days and did not like how it was adding up. Rachel started to believe that for some reason, someone wanted something from her or wanted to hurt her.

That was when it hit her…the book that Dolores asked her to keep safe—to hide! God, she felt stupid for not thinking of it earlier. That book must have something in it that put Dolores in the crosshairs and got Angela killed as well. It was probably the reason that the hotel room and the apartment were ransacked. *Someone must really want that book*, she thought. She had put the book into her purse after Dolores had left the salon on Friday. She did not even look at it. Rachel rummaged through her purse and started to dump its contents onto the front seat next to her.

Gordon saw used tissues, makeup, and balled up receipts starting to clutter his car.

"What are you digging for, Rachel?"

She was not sure if she wanted him to know about the book until she had a chance to look at it. Besides, he answered to the government and if the book was attached to Oliver Harrison, she wasn't sure where their loyalties would be; to her and her safety or to a mayor who was an ambitious politician wanting to hide information from his wife. She needed to have a moment to look at the book and try to see why or even if the information was worth killing people over.

Rachel noticed a sign for Paradise. "Where are we going?"

"To visit an Amish family. I know we'll be safe there."

She always thought it was funny that the Amish lived in places called Paradise and Intercourse.

Gordon pulled into the plain white farmhouse's gravel driveway. The stones groaned and popped under the wheels of the car. Gordon parked but let the car run. "Wait here," he commanded, getting out of the car and walking toward an Amish farmer that appeared in the doorway of the barn. Rachel noticed Gordon shake hands with the man and playfully slap him on the shoulder. It was a sign that Gordon and the farmer knew each other. They talked comfortably with one another and both men looked in her direction at the same time.

Gordon Ryan was full of surprises. She wondered just how someone like Gordon was friends with an Amish man.

Both men came to stand in front of Gordon's car. They shook hands again and Gordon got back into the car.

"Okay, it's all set. We're staying here. No one will know where we are."

"What, here? You are joking. Look, I liked the movie *Witness* just like anyone else. Actually, I think it was shot around her somewhere, but stay here? I don't think so."

"I am very serious. We have not been followed and nobody will look for us here."

Rachel remembered reading about how the Amish lived. No electricity, no modern conveniences. She went from her nightmarish life straight into hell.

His stern voice brought her back to reality. "We are staying." It was a command, not a question; not to be disputed. "Oh, and one more thing," he continued, "You just went from calling me your boyfriend to calling me your husband. Surprise!" Gordon gave her a slight smile.

"You have got to be kidding. We do not exactly like each other. I mean, look at us. You get on my nerves and I'm pretty sure I get on yours."

"It was the only way that we could share a room here. I need to keep you close. Someone ransacked that room for a reason. Any clue what they were looking for?"

Rachel was not sure that she was ready to tell him about the book. She had no reason other than she was completely overwhelmed. "Like I said before, I have no idea why anyone would be searching for anything that I have or know of."

"Why do I get the feeling there's something you are not telling me?"

"Why do you say that?"

"So there *is* something you are not telling me."

"Alright, as we were driving here, I remembered a book that Dolores Harrison had and it had something to do with the mayor's infidelity, I think. She asked me to hold on to it until she could decide what to do with it. She was very upset that that asshole slept with someone else again."

Gordon did not miss the look on her face. It was a look of anger and fierce loyalty.

"A book? What kind of book? And you didn't think to mention this before?"

"I just thought of it. I have been kinda busy. You know, losing friends, being forced from my apartment because it was a *murder* scene, fighting with my father and being stuck with you! My God, I know this is about the book now. Why didn't I think about it before?" Rachel continued to ramble on. "Dolores gave me a black book that she took from Oliver when she found out that he was cheating again."

"Where is this book now?" Gordon asked. "I should be the one holding on to it."

"I put it in my purse, but I got side tracked by everything else. I told you, I forgot all about it. The thing is, he was hiding the book."

"Who was hiding the book?"

"The mayor. Dolores said she found it taped to the underside of his desk or a drawer or something. So if it didn't contain something incriminating—either to him or to someone else—why would he need to hide it?"

"My thoughts exactly," said Gordon.

"Whoever is after you, must know that you have that book. And they are willing to kill anyone to get it. Give me the book, Rachel."

"No. I'll hold on to it."

"I will take possession of it and keep it safe, so you can just hand that book over to me."

"No, Dolores trusted it in my care and that's where it will stay for now." She knew she should just hand the book over to him, but she was not ready to give up her last connection with Dolores. Or some sort of control, however misdirected.

"Well, we certainly are going to the memorial service tomorrow. And if Oliver Harrison owned that book, you can bet whomever is searching for it will be there, knowing there's a good chance you'll show up. And they'll be checking out the salon next," Gordon announced. "In the meantime, we are spending the night here. I have to check in with my boss. You go in. And remember, we're married. Abe's wife and kids should be in the house. His wife's name is Sarah. Married, okay? Trust me."

"I have so many questions about this."

"I'm sure you do, but we'll discuss it tonight when we're alone, alright?"

She gave him a half-hearted smile as she opened the car door and walked toward the side porch of the farmhouse.

For the first time, Rachel felt like she really was into something too big to handle. Whatever was going on was all connected. It was not just a string of bad luck. Someone wanted information from her. The question was, who? Her mind immediately went to Oliver Harrison. Could he have killed his own wife? Was he even capable of killing his own wife? Or hiring someone else to do it?. Could he have had Angela killed as well? Could he have me killed? Rachel thought anything was possible. She had a sudden chill straight to the bone. Where would this stop? Could he kill Valerie? What about her parents? Or Shirley? Were they targets as well? Maybe he did not want his affair with his administrative assistant to come out. Maybe the evidence of that affair is in that book. If Oliver Harrison were running for Senate, he certainly would not want an affair to hit the press, especially when he had done such a great job of hiding all of his other indiscretions.

Rachel's mind was racing as she stood at the side door of the farmhouse. She knocked on the door and a cute little blonde girl with braids answered. She was dressed in a navy-blue dress and black shoes. She stood in the doorway just staring up at Rachel.

A woman looking to be about Rachel's age came to the door. She was dressed in a long, black dress held together with straight pins. She wore an unflattering black apron. But her eyes were bright blue and her skin was like porcelain.

Rachel already knew that Amish women did not cut their hair. They wore it in a bun and wore something called a prayer covering over it.

She assumed that this was Sarah. Her expression showed no impression of Rachel's attire.

"Hi, I'm Rachel. Gordon told me to come in. Hope you don't mind our dog," she said to the woman.

Sarah did not like having the animal in her home, but out of respect for her husband and Gordon, she remained silent. "It's nice to meet you, Rachel, please come in. My name is Sarah and this is Rebecca, she is my youngest."

"Hello, Rebecca," Rachel said to the staring child. She remained silent and ran to another room of the house.

As soon as Rachel entered the kitchen, her senses were overwhelmed with the smells of fresh baked breads, fruit pies, Whoopie pies and other baked goods. She stood there with her eyes closed, taking in all of the scents.

"Oh my, Go…goodness," Rachel said, catching herself.

Rachel looked around the spacious kitchen. The first thing she noticed was the most beautiful wood cabinets. Not the type you bought at the local home improvement stores. These were apparently handcrafted. The next thing she saw was a large, industrial sized wood table. It was filled with baked goods of all kinds.

"You made all these, Sarah?"

"Indeed. My kitchen is my favorite place in my house. I enjoy baking and cooking meals for my family. My husband and children are hearty eaters and they keep me cooking," she smiled.

"What do you do with all of these wonderful goodies?"

"I go to two different farmer's markets during the week. Many people purchase our baked goods and preserved items there. Are you hungry, Rachel? Could I offer you something?"

"No, please don't put yourself out for me."

"Nonsense, it is lunch time. I must feed my family. And the wife of Gordon is family to us."

"Well, alright, can I help?"

"Certainly," Sarah said warmly. "You can wash your hands at the sink and we will prepare the meal."

Sarah began selecting items and putting them on the table while Rachel placed Muffin in her purse then washed her hands.

Sarah handed Rachel a glass jar filled with applesauce.

Rachel thought that it was probably homemade like everything else that came from Sarah's kitchen. She was immediately jealous of

Sarah's superior abilities in the kitchen. Rachel could barely make toast and this plain woman in front of her could celebrate the wonders of nature and make things from scratch.

Rachel felt humbled as she began pouring applesauce into a bowl and placing it on the table. Sarah handed Rachel a knife and a freshly baked loaf of bread. Rachel took a deep inhale of the wonderfully scented fresh-baked bread. She began the task of slicing the bread and placing it on a plate. She spooned some apple butter into a bowl. It took all of her strength not to grab a slice of bread, smother it with the apple butter, and devour it.

The other items that were put on the table were chicken pot pie, green beans, and baked corn. There were a shoofly pie and a pumpkin pie for dessert. Water glasses were filled by an older daughter named Mary.

Mary found two more chairs in another room and added them around their table.

Mary looked to Rachel to be about twelve or thirteen. She looked as though she was budding into womanhood. Rachel lived so close to the Amish all of her life but she practically knew nothing about their lives.

Mary went outside and asked her father and Gordon to join the family for lunch. Two other boys came running out of the barn at the mention that food was prepared. They were instructed by their mother to wash their hands before sitting at the table.

Everyone was ready to say a silent blessing before enjoying a hearty meal together.

Rachel spent a wonderful day with Sarah and the children. She soaked up as much as she could about the family. It was the most relaxed she had seen Gordon since they had met. Even Muffin was enjoying herself with the children, which astonished Rachel. They fed her, took her outside to do her business, and gave her water. At some point, the bow came out of Muffin's fur and she looked slightly wilder than her normal pampered and groomed self.

So did Gordon. He looked right at home with the horses, the children, and his friend, Abe.

Everyone retired early and Rachel was grateful. She was exhausted and could not even remember Gordon joining her in the bedroom.

Sometime during the night, she woke to him holding and comforting her as Muffin slept at the foot of the bed. He gently rocked her as she sobbed. It lulled her back to sleep.

Monday morning came early with the sounds indicating that the household was coming to life.

Gordon was already up and gone when she woke. She went to the window and caught sight of him standing just outside of the barn door holding the reins of a mule.

Gordon felt her eyes on him. He looked up at the bedroom window and saw her staring down at him. She was wearing a modest nightgown that she borrowed from Sarah. It took his breath away to see her looking so beautiful. No fancy outfit, no makeup, just pure Rachel, and she was beautiful. He knew that the professional thing to do would be to look away, but he could not seem to do it.

Her dreams made her cry during the night and he comforted her. He knew it crossed many lines, but it broke his heart to hear the hurt that she was feeling when her guard was down.

Having Rachel Perry fall asleep in his arms was a mistake. Yes. But it was one beautiful mistake.

Oliver Harrison was smart enough to stop at a local grocery store before returning home. Carrying grocery bags into the house was the best cover he could do. A small group of reporters gathered on the street outside of his home. Cameras and microphones were aimed at him and they all spewed their questions at the same time, making it impossible to answer any of them.

Oliver was careful to plant the grieving husband look on his face before turning toward the cameras. He gave a small wave and carried the groceries into the house.

CHAPTER ELEVEN

The drive from Paradise to Harrisburg was too long for Rachel and Muffin. They stopped briefly at the outlet stores to purchase some clothing. Gordon didn't want to take the chance that the hotel might still be under surveillance by the killer. And their room was still a crime scene. Rachel picked out a black dress for the funeral, big sunglasses, black leggings, two bras, a few thongs, a tee shirt, jeans, and a sweater. Gordon got a few items and paid the entire bill. They stopped by PetSmart for some dog food, bowls, and treats. Rachel could not resist purchasing a little sweater for Muffin and then they got back in the car.

Rachel was fidgeting from boredom and played with the dog's new sweater as Muffin slept on Rachel's lap. There was a nervousness enveloping her every thought; it was exacerbated by the fact that viewings made her queasy. Rachel was also apprehensive about mingling with the Harrison family. Seeing an old flame after a few years was enough to make any woman nervous. Rachel knew the years had been kind to her. She was barely five pounds more than the last time Nick saw her. But she wanted to look good, play up her assets and make him wonder *what if*.

She was grateful for all of the makeup that she carried in her huge purse. She dug in the purse, looking for her favorite lip-gloss, and applied her makeup as Gordon drove.

Her hands shook as she applied her mascara. She swore under her breath as the car jolted and she hit the bridge of her nose with the mascara brush; leaving a black mark on the side of her nose. She dug in the purse and pulled out a crumpled tissue. She wiped carefully to remove the black mark and tossed the tissue back into her purse.

Gordon was alerted to her restlessness. "What's your problem? You're jumpier than I've ever seen you. And after all that you've been through in the past few days, that's saying a lot," he said, trying to start a conversation. "Nervous to see your old flame?"

She stopped in her tracks and turned toward him. "How did you know?"

"Oh, I'm trained to know. I've got you completely figured out," he said smugly.

"Oh really? I believe that I spend way more time getting to know people and how they think," she said defensively.

"You cut hair."

"That was hurtful. I do more than just hair, you idiot. You don't have to say it so demeaning."

"It's not what I meant. I mean you make it sound like you're some kind of shrink."

"In many ways, we are. A woman will confide in their hairstylist, sometimes before their own spouses. We know their likes, their disappointments, medical conditions, and so much more."

"Is that the kind of relationship you had with Dolores?"

"Of course. She was like a second mother to me. At one point in my life, I thought she would become my mother-in-law, but that didn't happen. It didn't stop us from sharing a wonderful friendship," Rachel said as she wiped a tear from her eye. "I miss her already."

"I'm sure you do," Gordon answered compassionately. He reacted to her grief and placed his hand over hers. He felt her pull away and instantly knew he was excessively soft around her.

"Sorry," he whispered.

"Oh, that's alright. I figured the tough guy act was just that."

"Just what?"

"An act. You're not that hard to figure out."

"You know nothing about me."

"Don't be too sure."

"Such as?"

Rachel was feeling smug and decided the conversation would take her mind off things for a few minutes. She decided to shock him with just how transparent he really was.

"Ok, smarty-pants, you are left-handed, you take your coffee black, you hate most junk foods, you like to cuddle in your sleep, and you had a thing with that female cop I met the other day. How am I doin'?"

He was a little annoyed that she knew about his relationship with Mickey. There was absolutely no way she could have known that. "How did you…"

"Know about the cop? Simple. I studied the two of you. It's a habit of mine; I watch people. I look for the truth in their body language and facial expressions. It is helpful in my job to know if they truly like the work that I do or if they want to leave the salon screaming; not that anyone ever does, but you know what I mean. Was she a quick fling? Too much to drink one night at a wild cop party?"

"She's my ex, we can leave it at that," he said through his teeth.

"Oh, I didn't see that coming. You really are angry about her." Rachel sank a little farther into her seat.

"Yeah, long story," Gordon answered.

"I've got nothing but time, Ryan."

"I don't think it's very appropriate to discuss my personal life with someone that I am protecting."

"Chicken," she said with a grin.

In a normal situation, he knew that she was exactly the kind of female that he would be attracted to. However, the situation being what it was, he could never explore those thoughts.

"Let's just say that sometimes even if you wear a uniform, you chase after them."

"Oh, she's a uniform chaser; makes sense. What, she saw your career moving forward and tried to jump on the bandwagon?"

"You could say that," Gordon was suddenly sorry that he even entertained the conversation.

"So what happened?"

Gordon decided that he was not comfortable with where the

conversation was going. His failed relationship was not a topic he liked to talk about. He never talked to anyone about it.

"Can we change the subject, please," he pleaded as he exited the highway.

"What's the matter, tough guy? Can't take tough conversations?"

"Alright, she liked *anyone* in a uniform. It didn't seem to matter that we were together. She ran around, sleeping with other men in uniform, which included my friend. Hell, she would bang the Maytag repair man if he was in a uniform. Are we done with this conversation now? Are you satisfied?" His anger was more than apparent to Rachel.

She began to pet the dog still asleep on her lap. "Damn, Ryan, I'm sorry. That sucks."

"Yeah, well it was three years ago and I'm over it. I was kidding about the Maytag man. But I'm over it, really," he said through gritted teeth.

"I can see that," she said sarcastically.

"Alright, what about you and Nick Harrison? What happened there?"

"Oh, college happened. I went because I was pressured from my father to go. I met Nick and we fell in love. Well, I fell in love. He saw me as worthy of his attention, because my father knew his father. Blah, blah, blah. The mayor, the money, you know. Dad likes his money. Business meetings and serving on boards and charity events for the rich and famous. They were old golfing buddies. My father wanted me to become an attorney and work for him. I wanted nothing to do with it. Therefore, I did some soul-searching and dropped out of college to go to cosmetology school. Nick was livid with me, because he wanted to marry me if I was successful in his eyes. Becoming a hairstylist was not what he would call a successful career..." Rachel began to sit taller in the seat.

She began to nervously play with her seatbelt as she continued. "Suddenly, I was beneath him. After many attempts from my father and Nick to wear me down and reconsider failed, he broke it off. He said I was not the driven girl that he fell in love with. In my mind, it took more drive to follow my dreams than to stay in college and be okay with the status quo. My father told me I was on my own. He said that unless I found a *real* career, I would never be anything. I lost the two men in my life all because I wanted to do what I wanted to do. I told them both to go screw themselves. Well, not those exact words, but you get the picture. There you go. That's my story."

"Oh. I'm sorry you went through that." He did not like that Rachel was put into a situation to choose between people and her career, it seemed unfair.

"I'm not. They are both shallow people who don't deserve my time," Rachel said as they pulled into the Miller Funeral Home.

Rachel saw Valerie standing outside, smoking a cigarette and watching for her. Even at a funeral, Valerie was all faux-fur and glitter. She wore black, faux-leather, skin-tight pants, a glittery, long black sweater and her faux-fur lined black coat. Her four-inch red heels added the Valerie touch and a splash of color.

The black cars were lined up for the processional. The parking lot was overflowing with vehicles and people. Gordon parked the car and they walked to meet Valerie. The viewing line was so long, they barely made it in the door and out of the freezing temperature. It looked like a stuffy dinner party. People of influence packed the funeral home. The place smelled of money and snobbery.

Rachel decided to let Muffin stay in the car and sleep. She bundled Muffin in a blanket Gordon had on the back seat and, as she exited the car, she looked up at Gordon, and let out a breath. He came around to her side of the car and squeezed her arm for encouragement. The intimate gesture did not go unnoticed by Valerie.

Rachel hugged Valerie.

"I see you still have that monkey on your back," Valerie whispered.

Gordon heard her and gave her a fierce look.

"Yeah, he's still here," Rachel responded.

Rachel was not the only one good at reading people. Valerie noticed that there was something about the way her friend looked at the FBI agent. Not that she blamed her; he was certainly fun to look at. Rachel was always more meticulous about her men. She saw something in her friend that made her smile.

"What are you so happy about?" Rachel questioned as they walked into the funeral home.

Before Valerie could answer, Nick Harrison descended on them and scooped Rachel into his arms. His sign of affection shocked Rachel. Even when they dated, he would do no more than hold her hand in public. He always said affection between people should remain private.

Rachel regained her footing and gently pushed away from Nick.

"My, Rachel, aren't you a sight for sore eyes. God, I've missed you," Nick said as he rubbed Rachel's arms.

She turned toward Valerie and Gordon to make her introductions. Valerie was frowning at him. *She apparently does not like Nick,* thought Rachel. She didn't like him very much at that moment either.

"Nick, I'd like to introduce you to my very best friend, Valerie. We also work together."

He reached out his hand to shake Valerie's hand. "Charmed," he said pleasantly; his hand-sweat made Valerie cringe. She never trusted someone whose hands were wet. It meant they were nervous or up to something. "Uh, yeah, hello. I bet you are," Valerie said, still scowling.

"And this is Gordon," Rachel acknowledged.

"And do you also work at the salon," Nick said with an undignified smirk. He looked Gordon up and down to try to determine whether he was straight.

"No, he's my boyfriend," Rachel said quickly.

Nick's smile was replaced with a look of displeasure as he shook Gordon's hand. Both men shook with vigor, both wanting to have the strongest grip. Nick was no match for Gordon.

Valerie let out a slight gasp, but Rachel ignored her as she went to stand beside Gordon.

Gordon took an immediate dislike for Nick Harrison and his sweaty palms. He had seen more than his share of the kind of arrogance that the attorney demonstrated.

"Well, Rachel, I see you've moved on," Nick said.

"Nick, it's been many years and not so much of a peep from you. I'm sure you've moved on several times since me."

"Well, sometimes you just don't know what you have until it's gone."

Rachel had no idea why Nick was acting so jealous. She knew him well enough to know he was up to something. *His mother is lying in a coffin in the next room and he's concerned with my love life? He's got something else on his agenda.*

"Again, all these years have passed. And I'm very happy now," she said as she grabbed Gordon's hand. Gordon saw no reason not to play along. In fact, it could be fun to play Rachel's boyfriend for a few hours. Anything he could do to annoy the pompous ass, Nick Harrison, brought him sadistic pleasure.

Gordon wrapped a protective arm around Rachel that made Valerie smile. Rachel only hesitated a second before she slid an arm around Gordon's waist.

"Yes, darling. Let's pay our respects," Gordon said into her hair as he kissed her on the forehead and rubbed a hand down to rest on the small of her back. He lingered dangerously close to her bottom.

"My, my, my," Valerie whispered. "Uh, come on, you love birds. They truly can't keep their hands off one another," Valerie said loud enough for Nick to hear every word.

Nick stood motionless, but his face revealed something Valerie could not quite place. She turned toward Nick and motioned toward the other room with her head. "Don't you think you should be in there with the rest of your family, Nick?"

"Very well, I look forward to catching up with you later, Rachel. I'll be in town for a week or so."

"Thanks for the warning," mumbled Valerie.

"Goodbye, Nick," Rachel said as the three of them proceeded into the viewing area.

Rachel stood nervously in the doorway. She knew that her beloved friend was no longer there and that the viewing was a formality for everyone left behind. Rachel never understood viewings. She did not like the thought of clouding her memories of Dolores with a picture of her in a casket.

Gordon's hand still rested on the small of her back. She could feel the heat through her sweater. Secretly, she was glad that he kept it there for support. The last time she viewed a dead body in a casket, it did not end all that well. She passed out on the floor next to her Aunt Maude's casket. She embarrassed herself and her father. His sister's funeral was not the place for such a scene…like she could help it. And she really didn't want to remember seeing Angela's dead body and all of the blood. She shook her head to clear it, gazed around the room, and swallowed hard. Rachel noticed that Nick reentered the reception line and stood next to his father, Oliver. Nick whispered in his father's ear and Oliver nodded in response to whatever Nick revealed. Neither man showed any sign of grief on their faces. Oliver was having a conversation with one of the viewers and Nick was staring at Rachel.

Gordon and Valerie led Rachel to the viewing area. Gordon noticed Rachel turning paler the closer they got to the casket.

"Are you going to be alright?" He did not like the color of her skin.

"I'm fine."

"No, you are not fine. Why don't we have a seat?"

"No, I have to do this for her."

"You do realize that she wouldn't want you to do something that you are not comfortable doing," Valerie chimed in.

"No, I got this. Let's just get it over with." She turned to Gordon. "Don't let go of me."

The impact of her statement hit him square in the face. "I won't."

The line moved and Rachel stood next to the casket. She was thankful that it was a closed casket with a beautiful picture of Dolores in a silver frame. The picture showed a younger, happier woman, full of life and dreams. She could only imagine the damage that was done by the bullet to her head. It reminded Rachel again of the scene that she witnessed in her own apartment. Angela suffered a fate just like Dolores. She was grateful that Angela's family sent for her body to go to their family home in Idaho and that she would not have to go through this for a second time in a week.

There was a stand next to the casket that contained various other pictures of Dolores. Tears fell as she viewed the many happy memories of Dolores' life. One picture stood out to her. It was a Christmas picture taken when Rachel and Nick first started dating. Dolores and Rachel were hugging and Rachel was wearing a beautiful new scarf that Dolores had bought for her. Rachel still owned the scarf. It was her favorite.

Gordon did not take his eyes off Rachel. That's why he never saw Mickey enter the room.

As Rachel turned away from the pictures, she caught sight of Officer Michelle Kinsley. She was dressed in a simple black dress that showed off her killer legs. Her hair was not in that tight bun at the nape of her neck as it was when they first met. It was long and curled. Her makeup was simple. However, her eyes were brimming with hate as she focused on Gordon Ryan.

Gordon was still too involved with the photo board and having Rachel by his side to take notice of Mickey. He knew he was taking the job of protecting her out of the realm of the investigation, but he could not help himself.

Rachel took a picture off the board and put it in her pocket. Gordon guessed that that certain picture must have stirred something within her. A new batch of tears was streaming down her cheeks as she turned to face him. There was no doubt in his mind just how much this woman loved Dolores.

Valerie hugged her best friend and whispered comforting words in her ear.

As the line moved forward, Rachel found herself face to face with Oliver Harrison. Neither could hide their dislike for the other. He viewed her as the mistake his son almost made. And she saw him as a lying, cheating bastard.

Their eyes locked in a knowing look. Rachel was well aware that Oliver never liked the continued relationship between herself and Dolores. As she came face to face with him, he suddenly became very charming; totally out of character for him toward Rachel.

"Miss Perry, it's so good of you to come."

Rachel saw something in his eyes. There was grief. She was beginning to think that maybe he had something to do with Dolores' death, but after seeing him, she was not convinced. He looked exhausted, distressed, but there was something else. He looked worried.

"Mayor, I am truly sorry for your loss," Rachel said shaking his hand.

"Yes, yes, thank you," he said, looking over her shoulder at Gordon.

"Mayor," Gordon stepped forward and shook his hand.

"Agent Ryan, I'm surprised to see you here," Oliver stated suspiciously.

The conversation got the attention of Nick. "Rachel? You're dating an agent?"

"Yeah, well it's complicated," she murmured.

Rachel began to drag Gordon away from the scene. Gordon nodded at both men.

"Mayor. Nick." Gordon stated as he walked away.

Valerie followed closely behind. They took their seats among the other mourners that were gathering to wait for the service to begin. That's when Gordon made eye contact with Mickey, who was standing next to Oliver Harrison. The closeness of them made Gordon continue to observe. She leaned in to say something in his ear and Gordon saw Oliver look in their direction. Gordon thought that Mickey was trying to weasel her way into the investigation through the mayor. He would not put it past her to try anything to advance her career in any way she could. If that wasn't the case, why was she here? She didn't know Mrs. Harrison so she had no business being here. Unless it was to see me.

"Ok, we need to avoid both of them for the remainder of the service," Rachel declared nervously. "They are up to something."

"Which one? They're both hiding something." Gordon placed his arm around Rachel.

The act did not go unnoticed by Valerie. She saw something between the two and smiled.

"Agreed," stated Rachel.

"Want to go say hi to your old flame?" Rachel asked with a hint of jealousy.

"Not even if my life depended on it."

CHAPTER TWELVE

I'm just glad that's over," Valerie said from the back seat of Gordon's car. "Thanks for taking me home. That cab ride would have cost a day's work. Do you care if I smoke?"

"No problem about the ride and no you cannot smoke in my vehicle," Gordon answered.

Rachel had not spoken since they left the viewing. She sat there petting the dog who was licking and trying to chew on the front seat. Gordon bit his tongue, though he secretly wanted to drop the dog off at the nearest shelter and never look back.

Rachel's grief was overwhelming. Yet, there was strength in her that he had to admire. Rachel's world had become a whirlwind and she was holding up quite well under the circumstances. He kept glancing over at her as they drove back to Lancaster. Valerie could not take the silence any longer.

"So, where are you two spending the night tonight?" Valerie questioned.

"A friend's farm," Gordon answered.

Rachel suddenly shook her head. "No, I can't go back there. I can't pretend to be married just to hide in their house."

"Rachel, we needed a place quickly."

"Yes, but today is a different day. I am not going to put them in danger or lie to them any longer. Figure out a place where we can go. Valerie, can I borrow some clothes?"

"Sure, come up and we'll hook you up. I'm sure some of your clothes are still at my place."

"Rachel, we need to disappear until the agency can figure this out," Gordon emphasized.

Gordon circled the block, looking for a place to park near Valerie's apartment. He pulled into a parking space and the three exited the car. Gordon scanned the area for anything suspicious, and for the guard that he had placed outside of the building. No cop car could be found and he began to worry. The girls made their way up the steps and Valerie unlocked her door. She was greeted with a beyond disheveled apartment. Papers were thrown about, lamps overturned, and her beloved couch was literally shredded. It was as if someone took a butcher knife to the cushions and removed the white cottony stuffing, then threw it all over her floor.

Valerie gasped in disbelief.

"Stay here!" Gordon commanded as he searched the rest of the apartment. He searched quickly and found no one. "It's clear," he stated a few moments later.

"Oh my God! Who would do this? My stuff! My couch!" she wailed.

"Valerie, Rachel, quickly get some things together and let's go," Gordon said with authority.

The girls moved about the rooms, gathering clothes, makeup, hair products, and shoes. They easily filled three large bags in less than ten minutes. Gordon was amazed at just how much stuff the two of them needed.

Valerie was still crying over her couch. Gordon thought that from the looks of it, it was not much of a couch *before* the brutal attack. He could not understand why she was so upset over it. However, he never could figure out what made women tick.

Rachel remained calm on the outside, but inside, her nerves were shot. She was reaching her limit and Gordon saw it in her teary eyes. "Ok, we'll switch hotels every night. We'll keep moving," Gordon declared.

"Right, that's a normal life," Rachel said bitterly.

"Look, once we figure this out and catch the person behind these crimes, you can go back to your normal life. Until then, you two remaining alive *is* my responsibility. So, let's get moving!" He was losing his cool. His frustration just doubled, now that he had both women to contend with and that was beyond demanding.

Just as the three of them exited the apartment, a police car pulled up. Michelle Kinsley and her partner James McMurray jumped out of the car.

"Didn't we just see you at the funeral?" Rachel said suspiciously.

"Yes, but I left early to get back for my shift. We got a report of a strange man hanging around here. A neighbor reported that they saw a gentleman enter this apartment. She stated that usually it was common to see strange men here, but not when Miss Meadows was not at home.

Valerie frowned. "Damn nosy Mrs. Beuller," she muttered through her teeth. "Always peeking out of her window and spying on me. I never liked that old bitch."

"Relax," Rachel warned, not wanting to miss the conversation between Gordon and Michelle.

"Watch this," she whispered to Valerie.

Valerie looked up and caught the tension between Gordon and the female officer that could be cut with a knife. Rachel and Valerie observed the body language, and the strained look on Michelle's face. And to Rachel's amazement, Michelle's partner, James was displaying signs of jealousy.

"Interesting, isn't it," Rachel said, trying to get her best friend's mind off the recent development.

"Oh yeah," Valerie answered. "Agent Ryan had a thing with the female cop and the partner isn't happy about them meeting up."

"His ex-lover."

"Really? Huh. Isn't that something? What is that saying about, "don't shit where you eat?"

"Yep, something like that."

"And the partner?"

"I'm going to say a recent lover or he has feelings for her and it is not reciprocated."

"Hmm. Interesting."

"Man, they really hate each other," Valerie noticed.

"Yep, oil and water. She's a uniform chaser," Rachel declared.

Gordon heard the words *uniform chaser* and knew *exactly* what they were discussing. That irritated him even more than seeing Mickey.

Michelle was not pleased that Gordon let civilians enter the crime scene, and from the looks of it, remove items from the apartment.

"Jesus Christ, Gordon, you know better than to let them trample on evidence! What the fuck were you thinking?"

"And where was the guard that I placed outside this door? Nice language, by the way, Mickey. Very professional. My job is to keep *her* alive," he said pointing at Rachel. "And now, I'm saddled with *that one* also. They needed their clothes and the rest of their junk to function. So, get off my back."

"I will report this to your superior," she sneered.

"Please do," he huffed as he marched over to his car. "Get in!" He was in no mood to argue with Rachel and Valerie and they knew it. They silently got in the car.

He sped off, swerving between cars. The girls held on and held their breaths. The slight headache that Rachel developed was in full force.

"Damn it, Ryan, slow the hell down!" she shrieked.

It was enough to get his attention and he slammed on the brakes, causing the car behind them to squeal to a sudden stop. Muffin practically flew off Rachel's lap and he slowed his pace, but his mood did not improve. He drove around, checking his mirror to see if he was being followed. Convinced that all was clear, he parked in the Princess Street Parking Garage that was adjacent to the hotel. He checked them in and they went to their room. Rachel and Valerie threw their bags onto the floor and both jumped on separate beds.

"Both of you pick one. You two can share."

"What, no spooning tonight?" Rachel's teasing got the attention of Valerie.

"You slept with him. I knew it!"

Gordon responded with a death glare that told both women that they were pushing it. Rachel liked getting under the agent's skin and decided to oblige Valerie's suspicions.

"Actually, Agent Ryan and I shared two nights in bed together, Val. You know how much I like handcuffs."

"You handcuffed her? Sweet!" Valerie fed into the embellishments.

"I did no such thing." Gordon flushed.

"Oh? I remember waking up to you spooning me and with your arm slung over my body. That hand just happened to be handcuffed to mine. Remember?"

"Yes, but that is not how it happened. There was no sexual encounter between us."

"That's a shame," Valerie chimed in. "You let a perfectly good handcuffing go to waste." Valerie added a clicking of her tongue and a shake of her head for added drama.

Gordon had enough of the two of them, even if they were just playing around.

"Ok, enough," he said sternly. "Let's just order room service."

"No, they have a great little restaurant and bar downstairs, I'd like to go down there," Rachel stated.

Gordon thought for a moment and glanced at the pleading looks on both of their faces. He let out a sigh and nodded in defeat. "Fine, but anything suspicious and we are out of there."

A half hour later, the three entered the bar. The first thing that stood out to Gordon was the look of the establishment. The walls looked like stone and the floor was concrete. The feel was very industrial and modern. The bar itself was in the shape of a U. Three couples sat at the bar, drinking and looking as though they all knew each other. Their laughter filled the bar and Rachel felt jealous of their calm demeanor. Her nerves were wound so tight, she thought she might snap like a rubber band stretched far beyond its capacity.

The bartender approached and he gave Gordon a smile of approval. One man and two beautiful women. The bartender liked those odds. He loved his job because he had constant contact with beautiful women. And he had a particular weakness for redheads. "What can I get you?" His full attention was on Rachel.

Gordon did not like the flirty way the bartender was eyeing up Rachel. But he never stopped to admit why it bothered him so much. He reasoned that anyone could be a threat to her safety and he was just being protective.

Valerie was the first to order. "I'll have an Apple Ale and my friend here will have a Margarita, on the rocks, salt with a shot of Amaretto. She likes her drinks like her men, strong and Italian." Rachel, who smiled, did not miss Valerie's long-standing joke. She certainly did not want anything to happen to her friend, but she was glad to have her to add some normality to the chaos.

"And for you, sir?" The bartender said, not even glancing away from Rachel and giving her a wink.

"Just a Coke or Pepsi," Gordon said with a warning tone and a look that could kill.

Gordon was the first to speak after glaring down the bartender, who got the hint and went to the other end of the bar to serve some friendlier patrons. "We have to get into the salon tomorrow. I had my team contact the owner. Told her that she needs to close until further notice and that you two will not be available. I have agents monitoring the salon to make sure no one gets in. It is the next logical place that he will hit. I'm surprised that it wasn't already hit, since he still hasn't found what he's looking for."

Valerie did not like the sound of not being able to work and she did not like being in the dark. "Hey, what exactly is he *or she* looking for? What am I missing here?" She looked pleadingly at Gordon. "I need this job. I have to go to work. Even more now that it looks like I have to buy a new couch," she pouted.

Rachel tried to reassure her friend and was at a loss on how to make the situation better for any of them. "Val, we can't work like this. Whatever is going on, we are both targets now. We cannot put Shirley in danger by being at the salon. Once we catch the person responsible, we can get back to our normal lives."

Gordon was impressed that Rachel was taking the situation seriously and it appeared that she was finally going to make his job a little easier. But he knew that he had to have a plan to catch the person responsible for the crimes. "You know, maybe it wouldn't be a bad idea for you to go to work," he said.

"I thought you said we shouldn't work," Rachel frowned at Gordon and began to nervously pick at her nails.

"Stop that!" Valerie snapped and placed a hand over Rachel's hands. "You know I hate when you pick like that."

Gordon just rolled his eyes and counted to ten before he spoke. "If we could lure the person out by having you both at work maybe we could figure out who is behind this. That person is looking for something and my guess is it's the book. I hope that's all they're looking for."

"What book?" Valerie looked back and forth between Rachel and Agent Ryan.

"Dolores gave me a book to hold on to. It's her husband's and he was trying to hide it. She wanted time to decide what to do with it."

Valerie could not believe what she was hearing. "All this crap over some book? Why? What's in that book?"

Rachel pulled it out of her purse and opened it. "A bunch of numbers, I don't know. It doesn't make any sense and I didn't really take any time to study it," Rachel defended. "Gordon, do you think that the person behind this is going to go to the salon today? Of course, you have no way of knowing for sure, but shouldn't we just get there and try to end this thing? He doesn't know that I have the book on me, so maybe he'll try to break into the salon and trash the place like he trashed our apartments."

"I think we'll be lucky if they haven't already done that. I think we should go now and maybe see who is looking for this book and why. You should give me the book, Rachel. We talked about this before and I let you have your way, but you should give it to me now. It will be safer with me," he answered and realized he liked Rachel using his first name.

They cancelled their drink orders and raced to the car. Rachel handed the book to Gordon who put it in the pocket of his jacket.

Gordon drove the two women to the salon. He felt that he could protect them both, but he did not want to linger too long. Valerie used her key to enter the building and the three of them filed in. Nothing seemed to be out of order. The posted agents must have been enough deterrent for the killer to stay at a distance. There was no doubt in Agent Ryan's mind that whoever was behind the murders was already close enough and surveying the salon at a safe distance, which meant that the killer saw the three of them enter the salon. He did not want to waste any time.

Once Agent Ryan indicated that it was safe to roam around the salon. Rachel took Muffin into the kitchen and got her a drink. She fed her some leftover cheeseburger, which Muffin devoured in a split second. Stomach content, she circled, sniffed, and defecated on the tile floor.

Valerie gagged as Rachel cleaned up the mess and placed it in a plastic grocery bag and tied it shut. Rachel was not the least bit fazed by the event and washed her hands at the kitchen sink. "Guess I should be grateful that she's not a Great Dane, huh?"

"That's not even funny, Rachel. I'm pretty sure it's not the worst thing that has ever happened on these floors, but it's still disgusting."

"Well, it's not like we've been doing a good job at taking her out to do her business. And I've been giving her a lot of water and food. What goes in has to come out," Rachel said as she witnessed Muffin squatting and peeing on the floor.

"Gross! I'm out of here," Valerie said as she went into the other room and freshened up her makeup and hair at her station.

Rachel cleaned up the mess and scooped Muffin up before she could do any more damage. She went into the other room to join the others and saw Gordon peeking in drawers and examining every inch of the room.

"Nothing is disturbed." He pulled the book out of his jacket for a closer examination.

Inside the cover was a small picture of skull and crossbones. "Isn't that interesting? I wonder what that means."

Rachel took the book from Gordon. "It's Skull and Bones."

"Yeah, I can see that."

"No, it is the symbol for the society at Yale University."

"Rachel, what are you talking about?" Gordon was confused.

"Okay, there is an organization at Yale University. It's called Skull and Bones. It's like a secret society. Although I'm not sure how secret it is. In the 1800s, a person named Russell and a person named Taft formed a branch of Skull and Bones in America. Russell became a state legislator and a general, Taft was appointed the U.S. attorney general and some other stuff I can't remember. They were men of power. Taft's son became president of the United States. Every now and then, there are leaks about who is a member of the organization. It is always people of power. Names like George H. W. Bush, George W. Bush, U.S. senators, and congressmen like James Buckley and John Kerry. Old American families like Rockefeller, Gilman, Phelps, and Sloane were supposedly members. The members take an oath that they would never reveal anything about the organization. They've supposedly been linked to scandals like Watergate, Iran-Contra, JFK's assassination, and other stuff.

"How do you know all of this?" Gordon was impressed.

"I had to do a report on government conspiracies when I was in college and Nick helped me research and write a report on it. He was a wealth of information. He even said that he had some relatives in the organization. I found it all very interesting so I guess some of it stuck. Who doesn't like a good conspiracy, right?"

Gordon stiffened at the mention of Nick Harrison. "Huh, good ole Nick helped you with it. And you never stop amazing me."

Valerie joined them just in time to hear Gordon's praise of her best friend. She was beginning to see a spark between Rachel and the hot FBI agent. Even if the two of them were clueless about it, she could see it. She noticed Agent Ryan glancing at Rachel every chance he got. Glances that were far more intimate than the FBI protecting a lonely hairstylist. Glances that said, I want you as more than a helpless victim of a tragic turn of events.

Gordon paged through the book trying to decipher the mystery behind the information. There were columns and rows like an Excel spreadsheet. Numbers one through six went across the grid and down the left side. Another column looked like it contained calendar dates. Listed in the columns below the dates were numbers. Random letters were listed in the margins coinciding with certain dates. He took out his phone and took a picture of a few pages within the book. He sent the pictures with a text to his boss. It did not take long before the hum of his phone told him that he'd received an answer to his text.

His boss stated that he had to rely on someone he used to trust. Someone who could never stop until he deciphered mysteries and codes: his ex-partner Gary.

Gordon and Gary Warbler had not spoken in a few years. Not since Gordon found out that Gary had been secretly sleeping with Gordon's woman, Michelle Kinsley. Gary was the reason for the break-up. His betrayal hurt Gordon more than Mickey's. He was his best friend; like a brother. Gordon never quite got over the absence of Gary in his life. No amount of time could heal a gaping hole.

Now his boss was going to insist that Gordon work with Gary to solve the mysteries behind the black book. "Shit," mumbled Gordon.

Maybe it was a sign. Maybe it was time for Gordon to put the past behind him. *After all, the past is the past*, he reasoned in his head. Gary was the best when it came to deciphering codes. But how did you trust someone who broke the most taboo of friend betrayals? Dicks before chicks used to be their mantra when they were teens. Broken promises and friendships all because of a woman.

CHAPTER THIRTEEN

Gary was stunned and elated to see Gordon Ryan's name appear on his phone. The text was short and to the point. *Need your help. Code to decipher. Can we meet?*

He was almost nervous to text him back. A lot was riding on him getting back into the good graces of his once-best friend. He had one shot to make amends and the time had come. God, he regretted sleeping with Michelle. Everyone knew she was a slut. Everyone but Gordon who gave her his heart. He messed up. He's never seen that kind of hurt on his friend's face before. The hurt was not that Michelle cheated, because he probably knew it would happen at some point, but that he was the one that she chose to sleep with. Gary had regretted that decision every day since.

Within a few minutes, Gordon received a text back. It just said, *Meet me. The spot. 3:00.*

Gordon knew "the spot" meant Brian's Brewhouse in Mount Joy. It was the place where they would go to escape. Brian's Brewhouse was a nineteenth century, intact brewery and hotel. It was the perfect spot for a private conversation over a beer.

Gordon and the girls left the salon and travelled to the small town of Mount Joy. Gordon did the usual scan of his environment to make sure they were not being followed. The three parked on a side street near Brian's and walked two blocks to the brewery. Snow was beginning to fall, making the sidewalks slick. A few times, Valerie almost fell on her bottom because she refused to wear sensible shoes. Rachel tried to convince her to at least wear some fashionable boots with a low heel, but Valerie was not having it.

The place smelled and looked the same to Gordon. A rush of memories invaded his mind. Thoughts of Gary's lost friendship, beers, and jokes; there was not a memory of his early twenties that did not include Gary.

Gordon picked a small table in the back of the Bar. It was dark and most of the patrons preferred sitting at the bar. Gordon took the seat closest to the wall so that he could watch Rachel and Valerie, who were gossiping at the bar. One of the locals looked harmless enough as he tried to hit on Valerie. Gordon knew that that guy was no match for these girls.

He scanned the dark bar until he caught sight of Gary in the other corner so far tucked in that he was barely noticeable. Gordon felt a pang of loss as he saw his friend move around the tables to take a seat across from him. Gordon shifted his seat so that he could still keep an eye on Rachel and Valerie.

Gary's nerves vibrated as he shook hands with Gordon. "Long time, bro." Gary caught Gordon's gaze glance past him and he turned to admire the view of the two amazing female specimens at the bar. The server brought the men two menus and sodas.

Pepsi was Gordon's drink and Coke was Gary's. They both studied the menus, but Gordon's attention was on the girls and their safety. It gave Gary a few moments to steady his nerves at seeing Gordon again. He knew he had to look him in the eye and despite everything, he did not want to see hurt and betrayal looking back at him.

His world went to shit after his brief affair with Michelle. He lost his best friend, whom he had known forever. Rumors spread throughout the station and the other police officers made his life uncomfortable. His mistake caused him to lose everyone's respect. The loss of Gordon hit him the hardest. He got caught up in the attention from Michelle. All it took was one extra glance, an innocent dinner while Gordon was on an assignment that took him to Virginia for a week, and he was playing house with Michelle. He always had a secret crush on her and having her pay attention to him was too much for him to bear. Gary gave into that temptation and had been regretting it ever since.

Now to get a text from Gordon that said he needed his help gave him hope that maybe he could get his old life back. Because getting Gordon back in his life would change everything.

They made eye contact but were silent for a few minutes, neither knowing what to say.

Gary tried to start the conversation as friendly and casually as he could. "Uh, you're looking good, bro. They with you?" Gordon kept looking behind Gary to see what had Gordon's eye. It happened to be the two woman at the bar drawing his attention. Gary was impressed at the luck his former friend clearly found himself in, if the lovely women at the bar were with Gordon. He turned around to look at them again. "Gorgeous! Shit, they with you? You *are* keeping an eye on them, I can tell. How did you fall into this one? What's the deal with the redhead?"

"She's off limits. Actually, both of them are off limits to you." Gordon fought back the urge to knock Gary on his ass. All of his anger was still on the surface and it showed on his face.

Gary knew that look all too well and tried to back step quickly. "I didn't mean anything, Gordy; I was just admiring the view. How the hell do you get so lucky to be spending your time with those two?"

"I wouldn't exactly call it luck," Gordon murmured as he and Rachel made eye contact. He nodded at her and saw her visibly relax a little. He did pity her. Her world had been turned upside down and still, there she sat, a little shaken, but strong. He knew it was only a matter of time and she would have to let some of her emotions out. No one could go through what she did and hold it all in. He knew that it helped her to have Valerie Meadows tagging along, even though it doubled his responsibilities.

Gary's voice brought him back to reality. "You said you needed my help."

Gordon cleared his throat before he began. "I have a book with a bunch of codes in it. The Chief…uh, I wanted your help in decoding it."

"Codes? Like numbers or letters? I am going to need more information than that. Where is this book?

"In a safe place."

"Well can you get it and let me see it?"

"Not here. I need a place to take the girls that is safe."

"Why? What did they do?"

"It's complicated." Gordon eyed the new patrons that came in. The girls were like magnets. Every available man tried to get as close as they could to the *trouble twins*. Valerie was eating it up. But Rachel looked as though she was ready to bolt at any moment. He had to get them somewhere safe.

Gary too was turning around again to view the girls. "Look, Gordy, I'd like to help you out, but you're going to have to trust me. I cannot play this talking in code bullshit with you and help you. You called me, remember? Do you want my help or not?"

"Okay, fine. Let's go to the cabin. We'll take the girls up there and figure this whole thing out."

"You, me, and those two, alone at the cabin?" Gary eyed Valerie from head to toe. "When do we leave?"

Valerie could feel Gary's gaze on them. She had a thing for men with dark hair and even darker eyes. His eyes fell somewhere between smoldering, dark, and mysterious. She liked the attention from the rest of the people at the bar and flirted freely, but the one with FBI Agent Ryan looked too good to be true. He was not a muscle-bound meathead like some of her past boyfriends. But she reasoned that muscles were not everything. She wondered if he minded smoking as she batted her lashes at him. "Who is the hot guy with your FBI guy?"

"He is not *my* FBI guy."

"Oh come on, Rach. I can see you have the hots for him and he is definitely interested in you.

"It's complicated."

"It's always complicated with you."

"Ouch! That is rough. It is not always complicated with me. I'm just choosy about who I'm with, that's all."

"You get any more choosy and you'll dry up. Except for the Dickster the other night, it has been months since you've seen anybody.

Rachel, you have to live a little. I know that timing sucks with Dolores and the Angela thing."

Rachel was losing her temper. "*The Dolores and Angela thing*? It is not a *thing*. Dolores was murdered by someone apparently over a book and someone tried to kill me and killed Angela instead! At least that's what they think," Rachel said through clenched teeth. "How do I ever stop looking over my shoulder for someone trying to get me? How do I ever stop blaming myself for Angela's murder?"

She took a huge gulp of her drink and glanced back at Gordon. For some strange reason, he made it better. She knew he was trying to help her and there was this small thing called *mutual attraction*.

Valerie downed the rest of her drink and winked at Rachel. "Okay, you are right, Rach. You have a lot of crazy-assed stuff going on. However, as long as we are stuck with those two hotties, we might as well have some fun. Take our minds off stuff. I'm getting ahead of myself. I assumed the new guy was joining our quest. You know what I mean?"

"Unfortunately, I know exactly what you mean. How can you be in this much crap and still have a one-track mind? The last thing I am thinking about is having an affair right now."

"Are you sure about that? I have seen the two of you together and there are serious sparks there. Any more sparks and you'll both be set on fire."

"That's not true, it's normal for two people thrown together to have some sort of connection."

"You two are like Lego pieces, you're so stuck together. I'm having a hard time believing that nothing happened when the two of you were handcuffed together all night and the night at the Amish farm, pretending to be married."

"Well nothing happened and nothing is going to happen. We are completely different people."

"What? You're both the same. Both of you are intense, sexually-frustrated individuals who are seriously attracted to each other."

Rachel glanced at Gordon who was listening to his friend, but staring intently at her. Not in a way that said, *I want to jump your bones.* It was more like, *I hope I can keep you from getting a bullet in your head.*

Gordon and Gary joined the girls; Gordon paid the bartender as he sent glaring looks to every guy at the bar as he introduced them to Gary as *a friend*. The territorial look he gave to every man in the bar told other males that the girls were with him. It was the equivalent of a dog pissing on a tree to mark his territory.

Valerie caught the look, shook her head, and smiled. Rachel was completely in denial about him. Anyone could see he was crazy about her. Anyone but Rachel.

CHAPTER
FOURTEEN

The cabin was located in Perry County and it was where Gordon and Gary would go to get away for a few days. They took their annual trout fishing trip very seriously when they were still friends. They were inseparable, Gordy and Gary. Brothers from another mother, friends would say.

However, Gordon was not sure if he could ever really trust Gary again. After all, he conspired with Mickey and it hurt more to have his best friend betray him than his ex-girlfriend did. *Bros before Hos. Wasn't that the saying?* Gordon no longer felt the urge to kick the shit out of Gary, so that, at least, was going to help their secluded cabin time.

They had avoided all contact since Gordon found out about Mickey and Gary. Now, he had to put the past behind them in order to figure out just what was going on. At least turn off the mistrust enough to get Gary to help him solve the mystery of the book and get the girls out of danger.

Gordon was distracted as they drove over two hours to the cabin. The girls talked almost non-stop and he thought it wise to tune them out. His mind kept drifting from Mickey to Gary, and every now and then, to Rachel's smile. She truly was a distraction that he could not afford to have. But God she smelled good and he loved the way she tossed that red mane whenever she laughed. He was great at judging people and he knew that under better circumstances, she was the type of woman that guys wanted. She was fiery and passionate and a challenge. However, loyal to those she loved.

Then there was Valerie. She had a pain behind her eyes. He did not know her story, but he knew that kind of pain. He suspected that her flare and showmanship was a mask to hide a lot of hurt.

That brought his thoughts full circle and straight back to Gary Warbler.

Gordon knew that for the time being, he was going to have to put his personal feelings for Gary aside and be a professional. It was not going to do anyone any good if he could not look beyond the past.

Gary was the best. There was no one better at deciphering codes than Gary. He was a natural code cracker. He glanced at Gary, who was staring back at him and struggling with what to say. Gordon broke their gaze first and reached into his coat pocket for the book. He handed it to Gary. "You might as well get started. The sooner you crack this, the sooner I can close up this case and…" His voice trailed off as he caught sight of Rachel in the rear-view mirror.

Rachel frowned. "The sooner he can get rid of the two of us. Isn't that right, Agent Ryan?"

Gordon did not answer; he only switched back to dealing with Gary. He was not sure that having Rachel out of his life was entirely what he wanted, but that was a complex issue that he could not afford to open. He had to just stick with the plan, get the girls safe, and solve this thing before anyone else died.

"I hope you can help us with this. It is your thing and all. It looks like some kind of code."

"Where did this come from?"

"I can't really discuss it. It's an open investigation that has brought the three of us together."

"Four." Gary looked up and smiled. "Brought the *four of us* together. Cuz, you don't get all the luck." He was not being sarcastic. Being strapped to the two women in the back seat seemed like a sweet ride. He glanced back at the one named Valerie. Her dark hair with those pieces of pink, purple, and blue hair made her look incredible. Her face was unforgettable and under better circumstances, he knew that he would be all over that. The timing sucked though, and he had a job to do, so he pushed thoughts of her out of his mind. "Okay, let me look at this for a while and see if I can find any patterns."

"Hey, when are we stopping? I gotta pee," Valerie complained from the back seat.

"We're almost there," Gordon answered.

"What's almost? I need a cigarette break, too."

Rachel was beginning to become annoyed with her friend. "Seriously, Val?"

"Seriously, I gotta pee, guys. Can we stop?"

Gordon reached a breaking point with her whining and pulled the car over. "Ok, we'll wait here but hurry up."

"Wait, what? I was hoping for a McDonald's or something. I can't pee in the woods! Are you crazy? That is just not done in civilized societies. That is why our ancestors created the toilet. I am sure you have heard of that modern invention. I thought you were smarter than that."

Gordon had had enough of Valerie. "Get out and pee or shut your trap. Either way I leave in two minutes! You pick."

Valerie got the hint. "Okay, okay. I will pee in the woods for God's sake. Like some animal," she complained as she rummaged through her purse for a few clean tissues. Valerie exited the car and began her trek through the brush in heels and she complained loudly the entire way. She disappeared behind a tree to do her business.

Rachel could not help but begin to laugh at the thought of her prissy friend having to pee in the woods. The sight of Valerie trying to walk as her heels sunk into the soft ground made it even more enjoyable. It was priceless. "It's good we won't have to hunt for our dinner with all the noise she is making." Rachel laughed and caught Gordon staring at her in the mirror. He smiled back, unable to contain it at Valerie's expense. "There isn't an animal within a three mile radius after her trip to the forest. I take it your friend has never gone camping before."

"She always told me that she was allergic to the outdoors," Rachel laughed. It felt so good to let out some emotions in a positive way.

Valerie made her way back to the car, opened the car door, got in, and slammed the door. "How the hell do I wash my hands?"

"Here," Rachel said as she rummaged through her purse for some hand sanitizer.

Gordon continued to enjoy the light-hearted mood and teased. "Is there anything in that purse that you *don't* have?"

"Uh, my mind. I seemed to have lost that when Valerie had to pee in the woods," Rachel chuckled.

"Ha, ha, very funny. Go ahead and laugh at my expense. But I swear if this cabin of yours doesn't have indoor plumbing, I'll murder all of you in your sleep."

The car erupted with laughter and even Valerie had to smile.

The route continued from Fox Hollow Road onto Route 74 and then traveled to Kennedy's Valley. Gordon made a left onto a private dirt road that was hidden from passersby, but was well known by himself and Gary. The two mile road led to another cut off and the cabin sat on a hill. The view was beautiful with the freshly fallen snow and the iced-over stream. The pond was just down the hill and both Gordon and Gary noticed that it was not frozen solid yet. It was their favorite spot at the cabin.

They each could not help but feel the pangs of nostalgia at seeing the cabin. They turned into a long gravel driveway and could see the cabin up ahead. Its wrap-around porch with a swing brought back memories where Gary and Gordon used to try to throw each other off the make believe pirate ship that was the porch and into the shark-infested water that was the grass.

The cabin contained memories of their fathers sharing hunting and fishing stories over cigars, beers and the longest lasting poker game in history, as the boys would go to the creek to catch crayfish and skip rocks. The winner was always the one with the most skips and the biggest crayfish.

Forever competitive, the two friends grew up learning from their fathers how to load their 12-gauge shotguns, how to tie on a fishing lure and how to exaggerate the size of the fish or the points on the deer. They were more like brothers than friends.

Their teenage years were filled with drinking beer and playing video games in the basement of Gary's house or trying to beat each other in a game of hoops. Gordon was taller, but it did not help him beat the fast and wiry Gary.

College came and went and the boys remained close. They shared an apartment while they were both at the Pennsylvania Police Academy and split the expenses, both working part-time jobs in the evening. Gary at Home Depot and Gordon at Olive Garden.

Now that bond had stretched to a breaking point. Gordon had every reason to be angry. Friends did not do that to each other. Even if Gary was secretly always jealous of Gordon, there was no reason to take what was not his. You just did not do that. He had crossed the line and the trust had been broken.

Rachel was blown away by the size of the cabin. She pictured a small one or two-room shack with no running water or heat. Instead, she saw a spacious, beautiful log cabin. It sat at the top of the hill in the mountains and the view was spectacular. The back porch area contained a large grill and benches. The right side contained a fire pit, wooden seats, and an old swing. The left side of the cabin was the stone-covered parking area.

Gordon pulled the car to the back of the house. Rachel put Muffin inside her coat as everyone exited the car and Gordon pulled the key from the hiding area inside the grill. He unlocked the back door and everyone piled into the cabin and out of the cold weather. It began to flurry as Gordon unlocked the front door from inside the cabin and stepped out onto the porch. He looked at the old swing, wiped the small amount of snow from it, and took a seat. He sighed and tried to clear his mind by inhaling some cool air into his lungs.

The sliding glass door opened and Gary joined him on the porch. They shared a look of yearning for years gone by; for a lost friendship and a fellowship that died a year ago.

Gary cleared his throat before he began. A nervous habit that Gordon recognized immediately. *People do not really change*, he thought. Gary still cleared his throat when he was nervous, Mickey was still a slut, sleeping her way to the top, and he still preferred the mountains to the city life.

Their broken friendship pained them both. Even though he was still pissed off about the affair, Gordon's heart was beginning to thaw. He knew that carrying that kind of baggage would never be good long term and it still gave Mickey the power to hurt him. That would never do. He felt a little pity for his friend who was clearly suffering almost as much as he was.

Gary almost looked as though, if he was not a tough cop, he would cry. He cleared his throat again before he spoke. "Gordon, I wanted to say that I truly am sorry for what I did. I hope that someday you can find it in yourself to forgive me. Or at least try to start over."

"Gary, we can't start over. We've been friends since we were kids. You've always been in my life since I was a small child. That would be like starting my entire life over. It is just not done. All my great memories have you in them. This place, our dads playing cards here at the cabin, sneaking their beer and going fishing. You steal your dad's car to take me to see that little Loretta girl in New Holland. So many things."

Gary looked elated as he brushed the snow away and took a seat on the top step.

"But I can try to put it behind us for now and see how things go."

Gary looked up with a smile. He fought back the urge to cry. People did not do that in front of other people. Therefore, he took a deep breath. "Thanks, I won't let you down. I'll be the kind of friend you deserve."

"Let's stop this mushy stuff and get our rods and see if we still have some beer stashed somewhere," Gordon said. "Nobody knows we're here. We're secluded and the lake is only 200 yards away. It might just be ice fishing. I doubt we'll catch anything, but hey, maybe a catfish will bite."

Gary stood at the same time that Gordon did. He put his hand out to shake Gordon's hand, but Gordon shoved him off the porch as they did when they were kids. Gary stumbled and could not catch himself before he landed on his backside. Gordon chuckled and it felt good to share in a moment with Gary again.

"You walked the plank. Now you are in shark-infested water," Gordon said as he opened the sliding glass door into the kitchen.

Gary brushed himself off and followed. He'd turned a corner and took a step towards normalcy again.

Gordon's laugh caught in his throat when he saw Rachel in his clothes. The girls were sitting at the rustic eight-foot dinner table, slapping down playing cards, giggling and drinking beverages.

"Slap! I won, Rachel. Hand over that Oreo."

"You didn't win, you cheated as usual." Rachel hated to lose to Valerie who gloated for hours at any victory.

"Come on, cry-baby, hand it over," Valerie said and turned and noticed they were not alone.

Rachel turned around to see what she was smiling about and saw the eye contact between Valerie and Gary, she knew it was only a matter of time before Valerie would be going on and on about being in love. It was a vicious cycle, but she understood Valerie's need for attention and affection. Her abusive past was textbook for her promiscuous tendencies.

Rachel caught the relaxed smile on Gordon's face and it made her smile as well. "Wow, you two look happy," she said as she sipped her hot tea and placed Muffin on her lap for some affection. She petted the dog who was perfectly content with the attention. "Hope you don't mind, but I found some tea in the cupboard. And uh, I found this flannel shirt to keep me warm." Her cheeks flushed at his admiration of her in flannel. Wonders never ceased. Men were so predictable. There was absolutely nothing sexy about an oversized flannel shirt, but he looked at her as if it were lingerie.

Valerie noisily sipped on her beverage. "I found some packets of hot chocolate. Wish you had some marshmallows stashed somewhere," she said with chocolate on her top lip. She licked it off and Gary thought it was the hottest thing he had ever seen. "I'm uh, going to look for some bait in the uh, the bait box," he said as he forced himself to turn away. Just looking at that dark-haired goddess made him hard. He turned his attention to the bait box that was stored in the utility closet next to the back door.

Valerie smiled in triumph. She loved seeing that type of reaction. It made her feel wanted and sexy. She knew the reason she craved that type of attention from men. Her shrink gave it some technical bullshit name. She had a four-letter word for it…rape. And the assault was by her beloved uncle. The dirty little secret that she lived with growing up. He made her sit on his lap in front of the family, too. "Come here, sweetie, and give your favorite uncle a kiss," he would say as he would force her through threats that bad things would happen to her family if she told.

She left home after high school and started smoking pot and drinking heavily. She tried desperately to drown the memories in booze and cloud her mind with smoke.

The therapist that she visited monthly to squelch her demons was only the second person with whom she shared her past. Rachel was the first. Rachel convinced her to stay in therapy and get all those feelings out. In addition, there was not another person alive that she loved more than her best friend Rachel.

CHAPTER FIFTEEN

The men spent three hours in silence as they fished. It was not the appropriate time of year for trout, but they hoped they would get something. They both came up empty handed and the weather was beginning to change to a steady snow, so they gave up as they longed for the warmth of the cabin and the company of the girls.

Gordon's phone ran as he approached the cabin. It was Mickey again. "Mickey, I don't have time for this. What is it now, Mickey?"

"You used to have time to talk to me any time, day or night."

"Yeah, that was before you fucked my best friend," he said as he remembered that Gary was standing next to him. "Sorry, Gary," Gordon said.

"What? Gary is with you. Why are you hanging out with Gary again?"

Gordon's blood began to boil. "Not that it's any of your business, but I need his professional help."

"So you need *his* help but you don't need mine. I am a way better investigator than Gary and you know it!"

"Well if I ever find myself having to find some guy in a uniform, I'll know to get in touch with you—because he's probably shacked up in your apartment, Mickey. Stop calling me." He hung up and suddenly needed to blow off some steam. "Let's go get the girls and get a beer."

When they were told they were all going out, Rachel tried desperately to calm her curls and Valerie was applying more mascara as the men were impatiently waiting downstairs.

"It's a bar in the mountains!" Gary yelled up the stairs. "Neither one of you needs this amount of fussing."

Ten minutes later the girls came down the stairs, followed by Muffin who had her bow affixed between her ears. Both men admired the view. Rachel had changed into another flannel shirt that Gordon wore as a teenager. It fit perfectly over her curves. She left two buttons unbuttoned and he noticed a hint of cleavage that made him wish he did not peek.

Valerie was decked out in black jeans and a black knit top that she'd managed to shove into their bag as they left her apartment. Gary could not stop staring at her perfectly heart-shaped ass and he desperately wanted to grab it.

Gordon drove them to the Bear Den. It was a small, smoke-filled bar with a pool table and a DJ playing 80s and 90s hits. The DJ announced that they would be starting karaoke at 9:00 and Valerie became overly excited. "Wait until you hear Rachel sing. She has the voice of an angel!"

"You sing?" questioned Gordon as he nudged her.

"Uh, no I don't," she answered sheepishly.

"Yes, you do, ya big fat liar!" Valerie scolded.

"I don't sing tonight, Val. Not in front of them."

"That's ridiculous! You are being stupid! Of course, you can sing in front of them. You shared a bed with this one," she said, pointing at Gordon, "and this other one will enjoy hearing your amazing talent."

Rachel blushed at the reference to sharing a bed with Gordon. She remembered waking up handcuffed to him with his strong arm flung over her. She remembered feeling his warmth and apparent manly bulge that told her he wanted her even in his sleep. That secret she kept to herself.

She looked up and caught Gordon staring at her. They shared a moment in the same memory that was pleasant for them both.

Gary sipped on his beer and tried to think of how to engage Valerie in a conversation. "You play darts?" he asked.

"I've been known to hit a few nice shots," she said.

"Well, little lady, how about we try our hands at some darts.""My pleasure," she answered as she stood and walked to the other side of the bar with Gary. They flirted with each other and Rachel could only pity poor Gary who was about to fall hard for her friend. They always did.

Gordon cleared his throat and tried to get back to a professional tone with Rachel.

"I'm sure we'll be able to figure this out now that we have the help of Gary. It won't be long before we can all get back to our own lives and put this whole mess behind us."

"Is that what this is to you? A mess?"

"Well, no. I was thinking that you've been through so much that after we solve this, you can get your life back to the way it was and move on."

"I'm afraid that my life has been changed forever. There is no going back for me. I'll never be able to go to the salon and not think of my sweet friend Dolores; I can never go back to my apartment without seeing images in my mind of Angela's death, which means I'll need to find a new place to live if I'm going to "move on" as you put it." She made air quotes to stress what she considered the absurdity of his remark. "I haven't told Val yet that I'm not returning to work. I don't want to put her through anymore."

"'Her through anymore?' You're the one going through this. Your friend seems as tough as nails. I'm sure she would get over it."

"You don't know Valerie like I do. You don't know what a shitty hand she was dealt as a child. She is actually not as strong as she leads people to believe. It's all a front."

The DJ announced the beginning of karaoke. Valerie raced back to the table and grabbed Rachel's arm. "You have to get up there and show these mountain hicks what raw talent sounds like." She shoved Rachel toward the stage.

Rachel caught her balance as Gordon began to smile at her and Valerie beamed, shouting, "Let's hear it, Rachel Perry. What does the next American Idol sound like?"

Rachel blew out a breath and slowly walked up onto the stage and gave her song information to the DJ. He took a moment to find her song on his computer and spoke loudly into the microphone. "We have Rachel here who is going to start us off with a little Sarah Evans. The song is "A Little Bit Stronger". Let's hear it for Rachel."

A few drinkers at the end of the bar started hooting and whistling at Rachel. Once she began to sing, the noisy bar fell completely silent. Rachel closed her eyes and it was as if everyone became invisible as she became engrossed in the song. Valerie's heart was breaking. She could feel the emotion in her voice. Gordon and Gary felt it too. She sang of moving on and getting stronger. *A perfect choice*, Gordon thought, knowing what she had just told him about not returning to work or her apartment. She was right though. She needed to remove the reminders of this tragic time. He thought about the pain he'd felt losing his lifetime friend for a year. He couldn't imagine the pain of knowing his friend had been shot through the head. And she had two of them. Then it hit him like a ton of bricks—that he might also be a reminder when this was all over. He would become a part of that pain and could no longer be a part of her life as she moved forward. Gordon did not know when it happened or even how, but he felt a feeling that he had never felt before. It was not pity or sorrow for all that she was going through. It was something more that he refused to give a name to.

He stared up at the woman with the voice of an angel and wondered how he'd let his guard down long enough for her to make her way in.

Valerie loved to watch everyone's faces as they listened to her friend's golden voice. She scanned the room to see the general awe that filled the room. Rachel's voice demanded attention from all who could hear it.

Valerie's gaze fell on Gordon as he stared in disbelief at her friend. Then she saw it. The look of a man in love. He was bitten and he never even saw it coming. She saw the internal conflict going on in his eyes. She hoped Rachel would be looking at him, too, so that she could see how bad he was falling for her, but Rachel was so deep into her song that her eyes were closed.

Rachel belted out the final note and held it. Everyone was wrapped up in her. When the song was over, she returned to being the same woman who did not like all eyes on her. She crept back to her chair, ignoring the tongue-in-cheek marriage proposals coming from the men at the bar. Then a gentleman at the bar took it too far for Gordon's liking. "Be my wife for the night," he yelled from across the room.

Without thinking, Gordon jumped from his seat in a blind fury. Gary grabbed Gordon's arm before he could proceed to the bar and break an arm or maybe a face of any man brave enough—or stupid enough—to continue hitting on Rachel.

Rachel looked nervous and Valerie grinned from ear to ear.

Rachel thought Agent Gordon Ryan was taking his job a little too seriously. "What's wrong with you, Gordon? They don't mean anything by it. Certainly, you cannot think I'm in any danger with those clowns. They're harmless bar guys trying to look cool in front of the rest of their friends. That's all."

Gordon knew he was being ridiculous. However, the thought of Rachel playing *wife* to anyone else sent his senses on edge. He had an urge to hit someone. He needed to find control and quickly. He took a deep breath and tried to relax the fists at his sides; purposely stretching his fingers wide and shaking them into submission.

"Okay, sorry," he murmured and sat back down. He might have been silent, but his eyes were screaming for anyone of those assholes to open their mouths again. He wanted so bad to pummel any one of them.

Valerie nudged Gary's arm. "How long do you think it will be before Rachel is playing wife to your FBI friend?" She winked and Gary got her meaning.

"Well from the look of him, he's already fallen hard. Like, fallen off a ledge, hit his head on the rocks below, fell into some water, and nearly drowned hard. I have never seen him like this, not even with Mickey."

"Who is Mickey?"

"Michelle. She hates the nickname Mickey, so we always call her that."

"Well, why did they break up?" Valerie inquired.

"I'm the dumb ass that broke them up. You see, Gordon went away and Mickey and I sort of hooked up."

"*Sort of* hooked up? How do you *sort of* hook up?"

"Ok, we had crazy sex for a week and then she tried to go back to Gordy. I had to confess to him. Trust me, we're both better off staying clear of her. She is what you call a uniform chaser. She seeks anyone that she thinks has power and tries to seduce them."

"Well, obviously your friend Mickey has had some issues in her past."

"You're taking her side?" Gary was shocked.

"Not at all. Let's just say that sometimes women sleep with men because that's how they think they can feel loved. It may not have anything to do with the sex, really. It's more about feeling wanted or needed. Other times it's because they've had a sexual encounter when they were young and it's what they know."

"You used to be a shrink or something? You seem to know a lot about this."

"No, I didn't used to be a shrink, just an abused little girl."

Gary immediately got her meaning and his heart broke for her. He would have never guessed that the confident, beautiful, sexy creature beside him had been molested as a child. He saw a painful memory creep into her eyes and in a second, it was gone. She swallowed it down again. He suspected that she had swallowed that toxic pill many times in her life. *What a brave woman,* he thought. *Stronger than maybe she realized. Anyone who could find some good in Mickey, or at least sympathize with her was resilient and thoughtful.* He had such an undeniable urge to wrap his arms around her at that moment and protect her from her demons.

"Time to go," Gordon announced with an authority that nobody questioned. They paid their tab, went back into the freezing temperature and into the car. It began to snow heavily, making their trip back to the cabin treacherous. No one spoke as Gordon drove. He turned on the radio to listen to the weather. They were calling for a foot of snow in that area of the state, and it would be worse up the mountain.

The winds howled as the snow blinded Gordon, keeping him from driving more than twenty miles per hour. The twenty minutes it took to get to the bar turned into an hour and a half to get back. It was almost midnight as Gordon maneuvered the vehicle up the snow-covered lane to the cabin.

Animal tracks could be seen everywhere as they scurried for shelter.

Valerie ran for the door, but had to wait for Gordon to unlock it before she raced in to stand next to the wood stove. The cabin was warm and inviting.

Valerie was rubbing her hands together over the stove, trying to thaw them. "Damn cold out there. It's not fit for a dog out there, my Pap would say every time he would come in from bad weather." She smiled at the memory of her Pap as she noticed Gary gazing at her. He came to stand next to her, grabbed her frozen hands, and rubbed them with his to warm them quicker. "Wow, you sure freeze easily, Valerie."

"Call me Val, my friends always do," she said, looking up at him with a look that could thaw a dead man.

"Christ," he murmured under his breath. "You sure know how to work those gorgeous eyes of yours, Val."

"Whatever do you mean?" she said, batting her lashes at him.

Rachel stood on the porch, wanting a few moments to herself before going back into the cabin. The wind had begun to die but the snow continued to fall and she silently watched the flakes as they wisped by.

Gordon cleared the small amount of snow off the porch swing and motioned for her to join him.

She walked over and sat down, careful to leave some distance between them. She sat tensely beside him as he smiled at her. "You don't have to do that, you know," she said picking at her faux fur jacket.

"Do what?"

"Be nice to me."

"I'm not being nice to you. I am concerned about you."

"I'm fine."

"I can see that," he said, nudging her with his shoulder. "You are the strongest woman on the planet. Now take your guard down for a moment and let me comfort you."

The simple phrase caught her off guard. She was not expecting the half smile and warmth in his eyes when she looked up.

"Not in cop mode at the moment, Agent Ryan? Not going to handcuff me again?" she teased.

"Only if it would make you feel better. Come here." Rachel melted into his strong arms and cried quietly as he rubbed her hair. Breathing in the scent of her and knowing he was crossing a professional line that he did not care that he crossed. He stopped caring about rules and what was ethical and started actually allowing himself to feel. He felt for her. Not the kind of big brother feelings he sometimes felt for people as an officer of the law, but a deeper sense of protecting and claiming something that he never thought he would feel again.

After a few minutes of silent bliss, Rachel was the first to speak. She slid a few inches away from him to look into his face. "I got tears, mascara, and snot on your coat. I'm sorry." She sniffed again.

"Snot, huh?" He straightened his shoulders and gave her space. "That could be a problem," he teased.

"I really do love the snow. I love the simple, clean look of fresh snow, not the dirty street snow that happens after humans start driving on the roads. I know, silly, right?"

"Not at all. I actually agree with you." He smiled.

"You agree with me? That's a first, Agent Ryan." She giggled a bit and it warmed him to the core.

"Come on; let's walk down to the water. I want to show you something." He stood and put out his hand for her to grab it.

She looked at the door of the cabin and back out toward the lake as she stood and hesitantly took his hand. It was warm and strong. "I'm not exactly wearing proper shoes for the walk. But who cares. I can thaw out my feet by the fire when we get back. I'm intrigued about what you could possibly have to show me at the water."

They walked to the edge of the lake and the only lights they could see were the brightness from the full moon, Gordon's small pocket flashlight's flicker and the kitchen light from the cabin. Gordon held her hand to make sure that she would not trip.

"Ok, Agent Ryan, what do you want to show me?"

"This," he said as his hands curled around her face and he lifted it to look into her eyes. "You are the most stubborn, the most difficult, annoying, wonderful, beautiful woman that I have ever met, Rachel."

He kissed her before she could protest. The second his lips met hers, a sort of internal spark ignited, filling her with a heat that could not be extinguished. A heat so powerful, it started in her belly and went straight to her head. One minute they were in peaceful bliss. The next, feeling the shock of the icy water engulfing their bodies and stealing their breath.

Then a powerful blast blew them both backward, knocking them into the frigid water.

CHAPTER SIXTEEN

Rachel! Rachel! Jesus Christ, Rachel! Come back, honey," Gordon panicked as he gently shook her. "Christ, your lips are turning blue, come on, sweetheart, sit up. That's it; we have to get these wet clothes off. We don't have much time. Come on." Gordon was yanking at her jacket and then her shirt. He was tugging off her shoes and undid the button of her jeans when she looked up and saw the cabin was blown to bits.

She was mumbling something inaudible as he wrestled with her wet clothes. Her wet jeans were a struggle, but he just managed to get them off as she bolted upright; terror filled her face.

"Valerie!" she wailed a blood-curdling scream for her friend and she struggled to get up. After two tries, she stood, found her footing, and tried to race toward the cabin.

Gordon grabbed a hold of her and stopped her. Rachel began to pound on his back, on his shoulders. "Get off me! Get the fuck off me! I have to save Val! I have to get to her. She can't die, she can't leave me, too!" She sobbed. Exhausted, she fell to the ground but got right back up. Rachel tried to run again, but Gordon was there to grab her and to keep her from running into the cabin. "Stop, Rachel. There is nothing you can do. Let's search for them. Maybe by some miracle, they are still alive." The words caught in his throat. He began to shake from the freezing wet clothing, from the adrenaline and from the sadness welling up inside him.

He didn't have much hope that they were still alive, but he had to go through the motions for Rachel's sake. Sadness filled Gordon thinking of the loss of his friend. Just reunited, working things out and now he is gone, too. Sadness for the loss of his father's cabin. With it, memories of his Pop in his flannel shirt, sitting on the porch with a beer in one hand and a fishing rod sitting next to him. *Ready to go, boy?* His thoughts were all over the place but he needed to stay grounded. Someone was still out there—here. All his training took over. He needed to get them warm and safe.

"Hey!" They heard a whistle and then another shout. "Hey! Over here!""

"That's Valerie's whistle!" Rachel turned and searched the immediate area.

"Gordy! Over here!" Gary could be heard and he was not too far away.

Arms waving wildly, Gary and Valerie came out of the woods and into the clearing.

Rachel ran to her friend. "Oh my God, Val! I thought I had lost you! Thank God you are alright!"

"I'm okay, I'm okay, Rachel. Thank goodness you're all right. When I saw the cabin go up in flames, I thought you were on the porch."

"No, we went for a walk. We went to the lake." Rachel stopped and looked at Valerie's face. "But where were the two of you?"

Gary and Valerie exchanged knowing glances, but it was Valerie who spoke first. "Well, we were in the living room, you know getting warm and we knew the two of you were on the porch, so we couldn't, you know make out with you so close. So Gary suggested that we grab a blanket off of the couch and go to the woodshed."

"You were making out in the woodshed?" Rachel could believe it. She was relieved and angry all at the same time. Not to mention freezing because she was standing there half-naked.

"Well, it beats making out in front of you, doesn't it?" Valerie crossed her arms over her chest in protest. "Give me some credit. I can be discreet, ya know."

"I swear to God, Val. I could murder you for making me so scared."

"You're one to judge. You're standing there with your jeans gone, no shirt, and no shoes! Nice bra, by the way. Is that mine? And where the hell is your coat?"

"Gordon undressed me because of the freezing water. You know hypothermia sets in if you don't get warm."

"Real smart, Rachel. Taking a swim in that frigid water."

"Oh my God, Val. I didn't take a swim. The explosion threw me in."

"Well, what were you doing next to the water then?"

"Kissing Agent Ryan!" She had not meant to say it. It just blurted out.

Both girls looked at each other, and had the same thought simultaneously. "Muffin!" They both screamed. Rachel began running toward the fire. She knew that Muffin would have never made it through the blast. She was just a little dog and probably was blown to bits.

Valerie was searching in the direction of the woods. "Muffin!" she screamed. Where are you? I let you out for two seconds and you disappear!"

Rachel heard Valerie and stopped in her tracks. "You let her out? Outside all alone? What were you thinking? Never mind. I know what you were thinking. You were thinking about how fast you could score with Gary here and not about your responsibilities."

"Wait a minute! It is not my dog or responsibility, Rach. You are the one who let her in the house and then decided to head to the lake without her. Did you think for a second she just might have to pee? I certainly did not want to be the one cleaning that mess up. So I let her out to pee and the next thing I know, Gary and I are hitting it off."

"Is that what you call it? That poor dog!"

As if on command, Muffin crawled out from under a nearby pine tree. Her coat was not the same glossy mane. Her bow was dangerously close to falling off her tiny head. She was shaking and scared. Her whimpering made both of the girls stop fighting and Rachel went over to pick her up.

Gary was not a huge dog fan; especially little dogs that look liked furry rats. "Are you sure she doesn't have mange or something? She's pretty rough looking."

"She's perfectly fine," Rachel countered. "She just needs a bath and maybe a comb. It's Valerie's fault she looks a mess. She was too busy with you in the wood shed!" she said as she snuggled the dog in the blanket with her.

"Don't yell at Gary. It's not his fault you wanted alone time with Gordon!"

Gordon had heard enough of their bickering. "Jesus, shut up, both of you! We need to get warm! Gary, where's that blanket?"

"It's in the shed." Both men instinctively grabbed their girls by the hand and began moving quickly toward the woodshed. Their neck hairs were up. The person that did this could still be around.

The footprints leading to and away from the shed were immediately visible to both agents.

"Someone was here" said Gordon. "Male boot prints. About a size 11, and judging from the depth of the print, probably about a buck eighty."

Gary nodded. "We can track him if we leave right now."

"Let's get that blanket and decide how we're going to track and protect these girls at the same time. We need a plan."

Inside the shed they found not only the blanket but some old work clothes: a couple of flannel shirts, pants, jackets, gardening gloves, tools, sacks of dirt, and a rifle. Gordon ransacked the counters and walls and drawers looking for ammunition.

They moved swiftly to the car. Rachel was so cold and numb that she never realized she was even in the car until she felt the heat hitting her legs.

Gordon took charge of the situation. "Girls, lock the doors and keep the heat on in the car. Keep the motor running. Gary and I will be back as soon as we can. If you see anything, take off, alright? Don't wait for us."

Both of the girls nodded. Valerie slid into the driver's seat. Rachel sat in the passenger seat. They were both too exhausted and angry to speak to one other.

The men were gone for twenty minutes and were pleasantly surprised when they returned to find Valerie and Rachel were sitting in silence.

Gordon moved into the driver's seat after Valerie climbed into the back seat with Gary. He placed an arm around Valerie.

"The tracks ended at the road. It looks like a car was parked there. The person walked in through the trail from the road and back-tracked when he left."

Rachel gasped and sat forward. "The book! Where's the book? Do you have it, Gary?" Rachel began to panic again. "We will never solve this without it and Dolores trusted me with it."

Gary sat in the back seat with his arms around a shivering Valerie. He dialed 911 and reported the incident as Valerie leaned against him, soaking up the attention and warmth. "It's gone, Rachel. I am so sorry. We'll have to figure this out without it."

"How are we going to figure this out without it? We trusted you with it. Once again you can't be trusted," she lashed out.

"Hey! That's uncalled for, Rachel!" Valerie reached forward and gave Rachel's shoulder a shove. "Apologize."

Rachel was sorry that she was taking her stress and anger out on Gary and Valerie.

Gary blushed. "It's alright. I deserved that."

"No, you don't," stated Gordon. "Can we just figure out where we think he went and get you two safe." He ran his hands through his hair and tried to concentrate on the road.

Gordon drove to the spot where the car had been parked. There were too many tire tracks in the snow to determine the direction he would have traveled.

Rachel looked behind her to the back seat. "I'm sorry, Gary, that was rude of me and I shouldn't have taken it out on you. You're here trying to help. Please forgive me."

"It's all good. Let's just catch this guy."

Valerie snuggled in to Gary's side and took a short nap.

"How?" Rachel's hair was still damp from the fall into the water, but she was much warmer. She cocooned herself around the frail shivering dog.

"Gary, don't you think it's funny that I get a call from Mickey and then the cabin is blown to bits? What do you think? Coincidence? She is the only person that would be able to piece together where you and I would hide. She's the only person who knows about this place besides us."

"Well, that does seem like a possibility, but why would she do that?"

"I'm not sure. But I have a feeling that the answer to all of this somehow lies with Mickey."

They drove back to Harrisburg in the storm. Gordon's mind raced to put the pieces together. Mickey was first on the scene when Rachel called in the death of her roommate. Mickey was at the funeral of Dolores. She seemed very close to the mayor. Maybe a little too close. Was that the angle? Mickey called him and knew that he was with Gary. She was smart enough to piece together that they would go to the cabin. Everything seemed to point to her involvement. Why? Why would she be involved with killing people when she swore an oath to protect? She would not be the first cop to have gone bad. But that kind of corruption usually happened in large cities, not in small cities and towns. He was missing something. He was not piecing another connection together.

"I have an idea. I know just the person who can help us."

"Who?" Gary could not imagine who was in a position to come to their aide.

"Mickey," Gordon said as he looked in his rear-view mirror at Gary. "She can help us."

Rachel stiffened at the mention of Gordon's ex-girlfriend. "How is running to your ex going to help us solve this? You must think very highly of her skills to want her tagging along."

"It's not her skills that I want; it's her appetite for sex."

Rachel became agitated by his comment. "So, I guess the kiss wasn't up to your satisfaction, if you want to go running back to your ex that cheated on you."

Valerie sat up at the sound of Rachel's anger. "I knew it! I knew you were making out with him! I saw it on your face. You can't hide stuff from me, Rach," Valerie said smugly.

Rachel became defensive. "I wasn't hiding anything. It was just a stupid kiss."

"Stupid, huh?" Gordon chimed in.

"Not stupid. Just a kiss. We were not doing anything uh, else. You know like making out in a wood shed," she stated and glared at Valerie and Gary. "And you! Wanting your ex-girlfriend! It is always the same with you men. All you want is sex. You think about it twenty-three hours a day. The other hour is thinking about food and bodily functions. I thought you were different. The way you kissed me, I thought... Never mind what I thought." She stopped herself from making any more of a fool of herself.

The car became silent. Gordon was analyzing what Rachel had just spouted off. It was true he was thinking about sex a lot lately. But it wasn't with Mickey. It was with Rachel. He let out a huge breath before he tackled the subject. "You misunderstood. I do not want Mickey for sex. That ship has long sailed. I think she's involved in this somehow and I want her to think we need her."

"That's brilliant!" Valerie exclaimed from the back seat as she reached for Gary's hand. Gary gave it freely to her and gave her hand a squeeze. He thought about Gordon's plan and pondered the safety of it. How much danger would they be putting the girls in with Mickey involved in their every move. "If you think she is involved, how will we keep the girls safe?"

"Keep your friends close and your enemies closer. We keep the girls close at all times. I mean glued at the hip close," he said, looking over at Rachel. She mouthed back a response...*sorry*. He nodded in reply and smiled at her. "I'll keep you safe."

It warmed her to hear the sincerity in his voice. She wanted so badly for someone to make the entire nightmare she was living go away. Someone to keep her safe.

They drove to his apartment to make the call. Everyone piled in the door and out of the brisk air. The storm continued to grow and the weather forecast predicted a foot of snow before the storm passed. The sidewalk was already covered with three to four inches and they made a trail as they walked single file into Gordon's apartment.

Gordon put Rachel's clothes into the dryer and gave her a pair of thermal socks to keep her feet warm.

Rachel noticed the military neatness of his things. No dishes in the sink, no socks on the living room floor, nothing out of place. "Wow, Gordon, you sure like to clean. Do you have a cleaning lady?"

"Nope. No need. I am quite capable of keeping my things in order."

"Yes, I see that."

"What's wrong with order?"

"Oh, nothing's wrong with it, I lived with Angela who was obsessive compulsive about our place. She hated my fringed rug. I would catch her combing those fringes with her hands and swearing under her breath, remember Val?"

Valerie attempted to smile at the memory. "Yeah, I don't mean to speak ill of the dead, but she was a nutcase."

"Valerie was always jealous about me having another person as a roommate," Rachel explained as she wiped a tear from her cheek. "Must be the cold," she lied as Gordon gave her a look of pity.

"Yeah, it's the cold, Rachel," Gordon said as he wiped another tear from her face.

"So, dumb question, why didn't you two live together?" Gary asked.

They both exchanged glances. Valerie's eyes pleaded with Rachel not to say her normal answer about Valerie sleeping with too many men.

Rachel decided to lie again. "We didn't want to work together and live together and ruin our great friendship," Rachel answered with a wink to Valerie.

Gordon dialed Mickey's cell number and everyone listened to his side of the conversation. "Mickey, we need your help. Can you please come to my place? No, I'm not alone. Yes, she is still with me. Yes, Gary's here, too. Yes, we're all here; now, can you make it? I have some information that I want your help with. Okay, in an hour." He hung up. "She took the bait." Gordon dialed a second number that resulted in a quick pizza delivery. As everyone ate, the silence became uncomfortable. Everyone was searching for something to say.

"How do we know she won't be sending a killer here to murder us all?" asked Valerie.

"We don't." Gordon went into his bedroom and pulled his extra Glock from under his mattress.

Ridge pulled in behind Michelle's car. He sat low in the seat, well hidden from anyone's view. Invisible even to her. She was dressed in her cop uniform. He always thought she was hot when she dressed like that.

Michelle knocked on Gordon's door and he quickly answered it. "You can come in," he said as he tried to swallow his disdain for her with a bite of pizza.

She quickly scanned the room to make sure all of the players were present. "Well, well, the gang's all here. I told you days ago to let me handle things. Now you need my help and I'm not sure I'm in a giving mood. What's with the mutt?" Michelle smugly went to the coffee table and snatched the last slice of pizza before taking a huge bite. She threw a piece of crust to Muffin who was already eating a few bites that Valerie had thrown to her.

Muffin peed on the rug and growled at Michelle. Muffin's hair stood on end as she lunged at Michelle's boot. Valerie picked up the dog, not trusting Michelle not to kick her.

"What the hell happened to all of you? You look like shit." Michelle announced.

CHAPTER

SEVENTEEN

Rachel took an instant dislike to Michelle or Mickey or whatever the hell her name was; who cared. She had a confidence that oozed from her pores. She had a perfect body and was not afraid to sashay around the room; drawing attention to herself as she picked up items and examined them with a few laughs under her breath. "You still have the same decorating taste, Gordy. Kind of a boring military feel to the place. And you still have the antique clock sitting on the table that I got you for Christmas that last year we were together." She rubbed the clock and gave Rachel a smirk that made Rachel want to pummel her.

Gordon saw the women glancing at each other, ready to pounce, and knew he should stand between them. A catfight would just set them all off. Mickey had just arrived and he was already tired of her. He took a seat next to Rachel on the couch.

"That was from you? Had I cared enough for it to matter, I would have thrown it away like all the other trash you left here." Gordon knew he needed to play her game, and to do that, he needed to calm down and keep it all in perspective. Mickey had a way of getting under his skin. She always knew which buttons to push. He wanted to grab Rachel's hand to steady himself, but he knew he couldn't let on to Mickey that there was anything more between them than a woman being under the protection of an FBI agent during a murder investigation. Rachel looked at him through a veiled glance.

Valerie had enough of the glances and snide remarks at her friend's expense and could not stay silent. "Excuse me, Officer Kinsley? Are you here to help us? Or are you here to be some kind of pain in all of our asses? Either way, let's get the show on the road so that we can solve this thing and get back to normal."

Gary placed a hand on Valerie's shoulder; a move that was not lost on Michelle.

"Oh, Gary, I didn't see you there. I didn't recognize you with your clothes on," she laughed and walked to the window.

"Okay! That's enough!" Gordon shouted and everyone jumped. "Are you going to help me with this thing or not? If you're going to start something, you should just leave; I don't need that stress right now."

"Relax, relax, I was just playing around. What? Nobody has a sense of humor anymore? Suddenly you're all serious and offended by everything. I'm just joking," she said.

Michel had been standing by the window, covertly watching the area, a behavior that was common to cops. She noticed the gentleman sitting in the sedan with his lights off; a car that she saw tailing her many times. She never let on that she knew he was there and he never approached her. She closed the drapes and moved away from the window just in case this night was the night that the stranger picked to try to kill her.

"Well, knock it off or get out," Gordon demanded. "Here is where we are. We had a book with dates and amounts in it. It had some symbols that we were able to identify as the organization Skull and Cross Bones. Are you aware of it?"

"Very," Michelle answered as she folded her arms over her chest.

"We didn't have a chance to do anything with it before it was blown up."

"Blown up? What do you mean blown up?" Michelle asked.

"We went to the cabin and someone tried to kill us. Do you know who would try to do that?"

"Me? Why would I know who would try to kill you? So far, you have done your best to leave me out of this. Anyway, so are you telling me that you lost the book?"

"Yeah, we lost the book," Gary said suspiciously.

"Well, I'm not sure why you need my help anyway," Michelle said. "You haven't needed my help so far."

Gordon began to pace around the room, but stopped as he made his way to Rachel. He needed to stay close to her to protect her. "See that's the thing. You were chomping at the bit to be involved with this whole deal. Why?" Gordon's voice was demanding an answer.

"Why? Well, it is an interesting case. Lots of moving parts and I wanted to dig into it. I am a cop. That's what we do."

"Bullshit, Mickey!" You are a lazy cop who doesn't like to do more than you have to."

"I wanted to get into detective work and thought this would be a way to do it."

"Another lie. I can see it on your face. Try the truth this time."

Michelle put her hands in her pockets and Gordon reached for his gun.

"What are you going to do, shoot me?" Michelle smiled. "I don't think so," she said as she took her hand out of her pocket to display the little black book.

Everyone was shocked. Gordon was the only one to speak. "It was you. It was you this whole time. Why, Mickey? Why would you get involved in all of this? I get it; you had to cover up the affair. It would have destroyed his career. He would have lost everything. We were supposed to think that it was some sort of conspiracy and that he was innocent. Do I have it right?" Gordon did not wait for her to respond as he drew his gun to point it at her chest. "But how? How could you have the resources to do all of this? You blew up my cabin! Two women are dead! You live on a cop's salary."

"I had nothing to do with those women dying! That was not me. By the way, I have more money than you know. I am very well off. I have enough hush money to retire on. I thought after the place blew up and the book was gone, that you would stop this, move on so I could just continue to handle things. Extreme, I know. But I knew you were not in the cabin at the time I was there. You were supposed to give up. Live happily ever after and no one else would get hurt. They were not after you, they were after this book. So now I have it and all of you can just drop this."

"You know we can't do that, Mickey! Cops do not blow up cabins and obstruct an investigation. Real cops save lives, not take them." Gordon became a human shield, placing himself completely in front of Rachel and nudging her toward the wall.

Michelle did not move. "Until recently, I have never thought about doing anything other than being a police officer. I am a good person, whether you can see that right now or not."

"All I see is a woman who sleeps with anyone who can make her feel powerful. Now you are going for older men, right? Oliver was an easy target for you. Powerful, rich and loves to screw strange women!"

Michelle's face distorted in anger. She'd heard enough from Gordon. She clenched her fists and screamed at him through her teeth. "He's not my lover, he's my father!"

Stunned, Gordon lowered his gun. The realization of the information hit him like a ton of bricks.

"Father? So you're not…"

"I'm not anything," she interrupted. "He made sure of that," Michelle said as tears of frustration ran down her cheeks.

"Sit down and explain this to us." Valerie said as she handed Michelle a tissue from her handbag. Michelle, finally broken, took it and did not care that it was questionable whether the tissue had been used in the past. Michelle sat next to Valerie on the coach and cleared her throat before she began.

"My mother was a poor waitress in Pittsburgh. She was a beautiful woman and caught the attention of Oliver Harrison when she waited on his table. He began visiting the coffee shop every few weeks. She had no idea who he was, other than that he was an attorney in the Lancaster area. He started asking her out and, being a single woman, she agreed. He would show up every few weeks for a night and take her to dinner, spend money on her, go back to her little apartment and make love to her. She had hopes that one day he would move closer so that he could work in the Pittsburgh area and they could get married and start a family. She was overjoyed when she found out that she was pregnant with me and could not wait until he came back to town. She dreamed that they would buy a little house, white picket fence, you know the deal."

Gordon moved to stand behind Valerie and Michelle as he interrupted. "She had no idea that he was married? Never asked any questions?"

"A woman in love sees what she wants to see. She may have had doubts, but she stayed true. Financially, he was paying her bills and got her a great apartment, so in her mind he was already taking care of her. She never knew she was a *kept* woman."

Rachel felt sad for Michelle and the memory of her mother. "Michelle, how did he take the news of her pregnancy?"

"He took it like any slime bag. He told her that a kid was not part of the deal and that she must have gotten herself knocked up by some other man that she hooked up with when she was whoring around behind his back. It crushed her."

"So sad," said Valerie. "What did she do next?"

Michelle took a labored breath to continue her painful story. "She did what any scorned woman would do. She got revenge. She blackmailed him after she discovered who he really was. She kept track of his dealings, all the information that he shared with her. His involvement in the controversial society. Everything went into this book. In a sense, my mother is in this book. His wife had just given birth to their only son, Nick. My mom told him that she would go to the press and his wife and tell them everything. He agreed to pay her. He paid for everything we ever wanted or needed. A trust was set up in my name so that he would never have to meet me. He wanted nothing to do with either one of us ever again, but he paid for my mother's silence. By the time I was twelve, she had drunk herself to death. But not until she told me the entire story. It did not help that she drank and took depression pills at the same time. She called them her happy pills." Michelle sighed.

"I found her, you know. She was lying in bed all peaceful looking. More peaceful than I had ever seen her in my whole life. She had a little black book in her hands and a picture of Oliver. She never got over him and I think she died still loving him. That is the sad part. She was a weak person who could not move on from him and make a new life for the two of us." Michelle hung her head and cried silently, wiped her tears, then contained herself again.

"I kept that book. I became hell-bent on knowing everything about the man who killed my mother with his cruelty. The book contained account numbers, transactions of money that he sent to her, and hidden in the pages was a picture of him. He was a member of Skull and Crossbones and I made sure that if anyone found the book and figured out it was about him, that they would see the symbol and know his secret. I have no idea what they do, but they have power."

"We saw the symbol," stated Gordon.

Michelle fidgeted with her fingers as she continued. "When I turned eighteen, I called him and offered him the opportunity to have a meeting with me before I exposed him. We met in a small town, in a small bar. You both know it well. Brian's Brewhouse."

Gary glanced at Gordon. "Yeah, Gordy and I know it well." Gary stood and circled the coffee table, walking slowly toward Michelle.

"Hey, look, guys, I am really sorry for everything that I did to ruin your relationships. I truly wish you both the very best."

Gordon slowly moved toward Michelle. He knew he had to disarm her. Gordon's eyes met Rachel's. There she was, standing with her back to the wall next to the window. For the first time, he thought they might have a shot at a true relationship when this was over. But first things first. He had to put together the last few pieces of the puzzle.

"Michelle, back to your childhood. Who raised you from twelve years old until you were eighteen and why didn't I ever know any of this?"

"I didn't tell anyone, ever. Well, except for my foster brother, Eric. He knew everything. We developed a close bond. One that protected us from the abuse of the foster parents that I ended up with. Nasty people. She was an abused homemaker and he was a drunk. How the hell they ever got approved to take in foster kids, I will never know. Every time the social worker came around, I was threatened to look and act like a happy child. They did it for the money, which he drank away."

Michelle took a sip of someone's water and placed the glass back on the coffee table. "Anyway, back to my meeting with Oliver Harrison. I told him who I was and literally threw the book in his face. I told him that he killed my mother and I was going to get even. I was not interested in using the information to expose him to the press; I wanted his wife to know what an asshole she was married to. Turns out she already knew."

"You spoke to Dolores?" Rachel spoke up. "When did you talk to her?"

"It was maybe ten years ago. I told her that her husband cheated on her with my mother and that she was dead. That woman was not surprised. She knew he was cheating and she stayed with him. She said something about keeping the family together for her son's sake and that she was raised that way."

Rachel nodded her head. "That sounds like Dolores. The last time I saw her, she gave me that book. I do not think she pieced your conversation with her to the book she had just found. But why would he keep it? Why not just destroy the book?"

"I think in some twisted way, he did love my mother, but like his wife, you kept the family together. She was just having their child, his career was taking off, and money was no object. He did say that he never forgot her and that I had her smile."

Gordon moved closer to Michelle as he processed all the information. "You were at the funeral. Why were you there?"

"I went because that was the second woman who loved Oliver and she was dead. Her death was under investigation. Not to mention that Rachel's roommate was killed. I wanted to help solve the deaths but you would not let me, so I took it on myself. I wanted it to be Oliver and I went there to threaten him. I told him that if I found out that he had anything to do with her death, that I would make sure it is known that he had an illegitimate daughter. That's when the asshole sitting outside your apartment started following me."

Gary and Gordon shared a glance and both bolted to the window. They both knew that looking directly out the window might spook the person Mickey was referring to.

Gary put on his jacket. "I am going to get this guy's plate info. I'll stay hidden, but I'll keep an eye on him." He glanced at Valerie before leaving the apartment.

"Any description, Mickey? You know who this guy is?" Gordon asked.

"Yes. I think I know who did the killing of Dolores and the roommate."

Rachel's heart flipped and she moved closer to the couch. "You know who killed Angela and Dolores?"

"I think so. I think it was the same guy that's been following me. Tall, handsome guy. I got a picture of him. It's a little blurry, but this is our guy." She passed her phone to Gordon, who looked at the picture and gave it to Gary. Valerie took the phone and she sunk into the couch. "That's John Smith."

"Who?" Everyone stated at the same time.

"John Smith. You remember him, Rachel. He was the guy who came in the day that Dolores..." Valerie's voice trailed off.

Rachel finally realized why Valerie stopped. "Dear God! He was in the salon the same time that Dolores was in. He must have been following her. He left before her appointment was over, but he was definitely there."

Valerie became very pale. "Rachel, he was also at the coffee shop the next morning. Remember we saw him there?"

"Yeah, I remember. But who is he and how does he fit into all of this?"

Michelle knew that answer. "I'm going to find out. I can only think of one person that would try to get even with Oliver and he would do it thinking he was keeping me safe."

Sadly, Gordon knew that when this was all over, even though Michelle was legitimately helping them now, he would have to turn her in for arson and possible terrorism charges regarding the cabin.

CHAPTER EIGHTEEN

Eric was involved. He could have gotten her killed. He was indirectly involved anyway. All he wanted to do was to get that book and blackmail the bastard that killed his foster sister's real mother. Why did he pick such a crazy fuck to get that book back? He knew him from juvenile prison. Grew up next to him in the same cell. They were like brothers. They swore that they would be there for each other any time they were needed. However, Eric never told him to start killing people. Just get the book and make Oliver pay. Making Oliver pay did not mean killing his wife. Getting the book back did not mean killing innocent roommates either. Rider was always crazy, but the fucker was going off the deep end with this. He could no longer be trusted and he was making a mess everywhere he went.

Ryder was too dangerous. He had a thirst for killing and now he was on a roll. Two dead women and he was still out there looking for the book. Rider stopped contacting Eric by phone because he said it could be traced. He stopped showing up at their meeting place, the coffee shop. Eric had no way to contact him. No way to stop him from doing more damage. Now Eric had blood on his hands and he did not even pull the damn trigger. How the hell was he going to be able to tell Michelle that he was involved? She deserved better than him as a foster brother. He was supposed to protect her.

Eric called Michelle for a dinner date, which meant beer and wings at the local bar. He dialed her phone and there was no answer. He tried again and she picked up. He could hear others talking in the background. "Hey, Michelle, I really need to see you. Can we meet up?"

"Oh, hey, Eric, I'm kinda in the middle of something. Maybe another night?"

"No! I need to see you tonight."

Michelle did not like the desperation in his voice. It startled her.

Gordon caught the worried look on her face and signaled for everyone to stop talking.

"Okay, Eric, I'll meet you. Is everything alright? You don't sound right. What's wrong?"

"Nothing. I'll talk to you when I see you. What time can you meet me?" he said desperately.

"I'll leave now and be there in a few minutes, alright?"

"Alright, a few minutes. I'll wait for you," he said as he hung up the phone.

"Something is wrong," Michelle said. "He never acts like that."

"Tell us about your brother, Michelle," Gordon said as he crossed the room, followed by Rachel.

"Not much to tell. He was my rock when I moved in with his parents. He tried to protect his mother from getting beat to death one night and he ended up killing his father. His mother blamed him instead of seeing that he had just killed a monster that continuously used her as a punching bag. She was so beaten that she required stitches above her eye, she had a broken arm where he hit her with the bat and bruises all up and down her legs. Eric saved her life and she wrote him off. He went to juvenile prison, and even though it was in defense of his mother, he served three years and was on probation for seven more years. That loving kid I remembered turned into a tough guy who trusted nobody."

"You kept in touch when he was in prison?" Gordon asked.

"Of course. He was the only family I had left. I testified in his defense and then I stayed hidden from Child Services until I was old enough to be on my own. After all, I had money. I got a fake I.D., lied about my age and rented a dumpy apartment over a Chinese restaurant. I used Mom's stash to pay for it. And when I turned nineteen, I entered the Lancaster Police Academy. I wanted to make sure that other kids didn't go through what Eric and I went through."

The conversation was abruptly halted. A shot rang out and Rachel let out a strange sound. She lunged forward and hit the floor. Blood began to soak the front of her white shirt. She tried to speak, but was unable to make a sound. Shock and fear showed in her eyes as Valerie and Gordon appeared in her line of vision before she passed out.

Valerie knelt and laid Rachel's lifeless head on her lap and cradled her. She pulled her hand from under Rachel and saw the blood all over her hand. The bright crimson lifeblood trickled onto the floor.

"Jesus! Call 911! Rachel's been shot!"

Gary came running into the apartment. "I couldn't get to him fast enough. He shot from inside the car and then he took off. I hope he…"

The scene in front of Gary played out like an action movie. There was a bleeding woman on the floor, both Valerie and Gordon were bent over her, and Michelle's hands were covering her opened mouth.

"We can't wait! She is losing too much blood," Gordon yelled.

Gary was the first person out the door, followed by Michelle. They went into cop mode as they searched the perimeter. They confirmed that the shooter seemed to have disappeared and didn't circle back. Knowing that it appeared to be safe for the moment, Gary and Michelle ran to Gordon's car to prepare to move Rachel and get her to the hospital. Gary opened the passenger side door to make things easier for Gordon. Michelle jumped into the back seat and continued to scan for any signs of John Smith or whoever he was. She was feeling so much guilt that she might have cost Rachel her life. Instead of protecting her, she might have inadvertently gotten her killed.

Gordon did not waste any time. He scooped Rachel into his arms and carried her to the car. Valerie was openly sobbing and trying to hold onto Muffin. She dumped out Rachel's purse contents and placed Muffin inside with some kibble, grabbed a water bottle from the coffee table and slammed the door behind her. She was glad she thought of the purse so that she could conceal Muffin in the emergency room. It was almost as if Muffin knew what was going on because she was silent and stayed in the purse. Still, Valerie felt the need to give her a warning. "Devil dog, you better not be any trouble, or the next step will be the pound. Got it?" Valerie muttered into the purse.

Gordon ran to the car and placed Rachel into the back seat then ran around and got in beside her. He cradled Rachel and applied pressure to her wound. Gary drove Gordon's car. Valerie was in the back seat on the other side of Rachel.

Michelle drove her police car with the sirens blaring and the lights flashing to clear the way for Gary to drive as fast as possible. They raced to the hospital located four blocks away.

Gary pulled into the ER parking lot.

Gordon jumped out and carried Rachel in through the exterior doors, and went straight through the ER doors. He placed Rachel on the gurney that was being pushed toward them by a nurse and an orderly. Valerie ran behind him.

"Gunshot to the back," he stated flatly.

Within minutes, Rachel was being whisked off to emergency surgery. Gordon, Michelle, Valerie and Gary sat in the waiting room in numbed silence. Valerie saw her neighbor Taz entering the doors and practically tackled him as she rushed to him. "Taz," she said as she fell into his arms and sobbed.

Taz was unaware of what happened. He pulled Valerie away from his body so that he could examine her face. "Valerie, sit down and tell me what's wrong."

"It's Rach! She's been shot. God, Taz, please find out something. Please save her!"

Taz felt stunned by the news, but he put on his *doctor face* to deal with both the patient that he happened to be infatuated with, and his dear friend Valerie, whose heart was breaking. "Val, please stay calm for Rachel's sake. I'll go and check on her status. I promise to do everything that I can for her… for you. You know I will."

"I know you will, Taz." Valerie found comfort in Gary's arms and sobbed into his shirt while Gordon paced back and forth. She found a tissue in the front pocket of Rachel's purse and blew her nose in it.

"Don't worry, Agent Ryan. Taz will make sure Rachel is alright. He has to. I have known him almost all my life. He is a good guy and he secretly has a major crush on Rachel, even though she doesn't give him the time of day. He still pines for her and so he's going to make sure she comes out of this alright."

Gary thought it best to keep Valerie talking and distracted. "You said you have known this Taz guy for a long time. How did you meet?"

"Third grade. He was trying to lift the skirt of my friend's dress and I clocked him. We both were sent to the principal's office and we bonded over our fear of Mrs. Allister. She was one mean bitch. Why she chose to work with children, nobody knew. She obviously hated all people under five feet. So Taz and I were in trouble a lot and vowed to try to keep each other out of trouble and out of the clutches of Mrs. Allister."

"Is Taz his real name? Nickname?"

"Yeah, that started in High School. He was a track star. Nobody could beat him. He was nicknamed the Tasmanian devil…Taz for short. He was out of control when he ran. He won all kinds of titles and awards. The nickname stuck. His real name is Tom Anderton. Boring Tom Anderton. When an apartment became vacant in my building, I called him and told him about it and now he's my friend as well as my neighbor. He's pretty cool. He thinks he's in love with Rachel and she doesn't like him in that way. So I know he'll do anything to keep her alive. I trust him to do everything he can for her. Sorry I forgot to introduce you, Gary."

"Valerie, it's alright. I don't get jealous like that. And I don't have a claim on you…well, not yet anyways." He held her close and she leaned into his strength.

Gordon had never been more scared in this life. Why did he have to go and be messed up with Rachel? He was perfectly happy being alone. When she was not arguing with him, she was teasing him. He lowered his gaze to the front of his shirt. It had her blood all over it. A lot of it. The thought of losing her was making him nauseated.

Michelle could see the anguish on Gordon's face and felt entirely responsible for the shooting. "Gordon, this is my fault. I think that bullet was intended for me. This guy has been following me as I told you. Maybe he wanted to kill me. What can I do? I have to help."

"Mickey, uh um, Michelle, you can help. Have that dinner with your brother. Try to find out what he knows."

"Okay. I'll find out what I can and come right back here. Gordy, I'm really sorry," she said as a tear slipped down her cheek. There was so much that she was sorry for. So many people she had hurt or taken for granted. So much time wasted when she could have tried to have a normal life, whatever that was. Instead, she ruined every good thing that came her way. At some point, a person had to stop blaming all the things they screwed up in their lives on their shitty childhood. Stop blaming others and start fixing what was wrong with them.

Michelle drove to the bar and parked next to her brother's car. Thank goodness he waited. She entered the dimly lit, smoke-filled bar and squinted to find her foster brother shooting pool with a woman whose jeans were so tight, Michelle wondered how she could bend forward to bank a shot into the corner pocket.

Eric scanned the room and made eye contact with Michelle. He grinned as he winked at her and motioned for her to have a seat next to the back wall of the bar. She saw his favorite brand of cigarettes and half a beer. *Some things never change*, she thought. Her heart would break if he was involved with the murders. He was the only true thing in her life. She took a seat as he sunk the eight ball into the pocket he called.

Rachel could hear mumbling, but she was having trouble opening her eyes. She heard a sob from a familiar voice, yet she was unable to stir.

"Rachel, it's Mom. Please open your eyes, please. You are scaring your father and me to death. Maria is here, too. She is worried sick," Margaret sobbed as she pulled a tissue out of her purse and wiped her tears away. She rose from the side of the bed and quietly moved to the foot of the bed and began to absently rub Rachel's feet. "She loved this as a child. It would always make her smile."

Maria placed a protective arm around Margaret and wiped her own tears away.

Mitchell Perry cleared his throat and walked to the side where his wife had just left. Standing tall and strong, he willed her to wake up. She looked small and pale. It broke him when he realized that the last conversation that they had was in anger. Unable to remain strong, he sat and immediately grabbed Rachel's hand. "Rachel, you are upsetting your mother. And, um, me," he said as a lump in his throat prevented him from continuing without a sip of water to choke it down. "Rachel, I am sorry. Maybe if I had listened to you. Maybe if I had made your life choices acceptable, you wouldn't have gotten mixed up in all of this. Agent Ryan told us everything. He said you have been very brave and I think he is very fond of you." He brought her hand to his lips. "Please, wake up, Rachel. I love you."

Mitchell stood to pace the room as a nurse came in to inform everyone that visiting hours were over and that they just needed to give her time to wake up.

"Daddy?" Rachel's eyes fluttered open. "Mom? Where am I?" She scanned the room and her eyes met Gordon's look of anxiety. "I was shot, wasn't I?" He nodded his head, as he remained composed. Inside he felt as if he finally took a breath after ten long hours of waiting for Rachel to stir.

Valerie tore away from Gary and practically laid across Rachel. "Jesus, Rach, you scared the hell out of me. Thank God you're awake and alive!"

"Val, I can't breathe!" Rachel mumbled into Valerie's shoulder.

"Sorry, sorry. I'm just so glad you're alive. I thought I lost you." She kissed Rachel's cheek and moved aside to allow Rachel's parents to be close to their daughter.

Rachel sobbed as her father held her close, whispering how sorry he was and how much he loved her. "It's okay, Daddy. You and I will now fix us and communicate better. I'm sorry, too. I get my stubborn streak from you," she teased.

The nurse was quick to clear everyone from the room. "She needs her rest. You can all come back in the morning."

Mitchell promised to return in the morning and hoped to be able to take their daughter home to heal.

Valerie and Gary left together in a taxi. Gordon used his FBI status to stay. He was still charged with protecting her. The gunman was still out there, and whether that bullet was meant for Michelle or Rachel, it was his responsibility to protect her until it was all over. He called for a police guard to be posted outside her door round the clock.

He sat beside her bed, stroking her hair and was no longer able to hide his feelings for her. He saw it in her face that she was feeling the same connection to him. They had been thrown together, so it was natural for them to feel a connection.

He sat in silence and rubbed her head until she fell asleep. She looked pale and small, but thank God, she was alive. He could not help but feel guilty. He promised to keep her safe, but he had failed. He watched her sleeping, watching the slow rhythm of her breathing, and prayed that she would recover quickly.

Eric finished his game of pool and slapped the woman who beat him on the ass. He walked over to the table and kissed his foster sister on the cheek. "Wow, you get more beautiful every day, Sis. How have you been? I'm glad you finally answered my call."

Michelle felt frazzled and out of control. She did not know exactly how to approach the subject of his potential involvement in the murders. "Hi, Eric, how have you been?" she said, leaning in to kiss his cheek.

"Good, Sis. I had to see you. Had to make sure that you were okay."

"Yeah, I'm okay. Eric, remember when we always said that we would keep each other out of trouble?"

"Yes."

"Have you been doing anything that might have put me in trouble?"

"Look, Michelle. I will always be responsible for you. I will always protect you. You are my whole family. My whole life."

"Eric, please tell me. What is going on? What did you do?"

Eric shifted in his seat and took a gulp of his beer before he answered. He leaned in to whisper to her.

"I know you wanted the book back. I know Oliver had it. When his wife found it and he realized that it was gone, he wanted me to find the book. I had done jobs for him before, and he paid very well."

"Eric, how could you work for the man who was the reason for my mom's death and my misery?" Michelle was angry, but tried to remain calm so that she could get the whole story from Eric.

"Because he thought either you or Dolores Harrison took it and tried to find someone else to get rid of you once and for all if it was in your possession. He knew because you grew up with me, that if you had the book again, I could get it and he could destroy it."

"If he wanted it destroyed, why didn't he do it when he had it?"

Eric shrugged his shoulders. "Beats me. All I know is that he wants you dead. I cannot let that happen. I took the job to get the book and I was going to negotiate with him to not go after you. I used one of my acquaintances from juvy. He was supposed to first follow Dolores and make sure she didn't have it. When Dolores went to the salon, he also went in and assumed that Dolores could have passed it on to Rachel Perry. He murdered Dolores, which I never told him to do. I only wanted him to get the book so that Oliver would not try to kill you for being his daughter. He was running for Senator and could not have his illegitimate child showing up during the election. The next thing my associate Rider did was search Rachel's apartment. He again went rogue. He killed the roommate. He's skittish and out of control."

Duty over family. Michelle excused herself to the bathroom and dialed for police back up. It was too much for her to bear. She knew he needed to be arrested for breaking the law. Michelle was torn, but she made a vow to uphold the law and that could not be negotiated. She had to live with the fact that she torched Gordon's cabin and hoped that he would not have her arrested for it. Murder of Rachel's friends was not something forgivable.

She stalled in the bathroom and cringed as she heard the ruckus going on in the bar area.

"Michelle! Michelle! How could you?" Eric screamed her name over and over again. It was just too much for her and she sobbed as she exited the bathroom while they were loading him into the police car, still screaming her name.

CHAPTER
NINETEEN

Valerie borrowed Gary's car to go to see Rachel and Gordon's new home. Technically, it was also her car, but since they were now living together, he told her to use it any time that she wanted. The ring on her finger told her she was loved and that made her very happy. And having Muffin as a pet was almost like having a child. She was glad that Rachel decided to part with Muffin, since she secretly always liked the little pooch.

As she pulled up to the curb, she saw Gordon's car was gone, but Rachel's used Audi was in the driveway.

She couldn't help but notice how hard Rachel was working on her garden. The flowers were blooming and full of life. Just like Rachel.

She walked in the front door and called for Rachel without an answer. The aroma of fresh coffee filled the house. Valerie poured herself a cup and followed the sound of Adele crooning about a lost love. As she approached one of the bedrooms, she could hear Rachel singing along and killing every note. What talent her friend had.

Not wanting to scare Rachel, she slowly opened the bedroom door to find Rachel standing on a ladder and painting the walls a pretty pale pink.

"Jesus, Rach, should you be up there doing that in your condition? Gordon would kill you if he knew you were on a ladder."

"I'm having a baby, Val. It is not a condition. Women all over the world from the beginning of time have been having babies and they did more than just paint a room."

"Are you nesting?" Valerie asked as she sipped on her coffee.

"Am I what?" Rachel stopped long enough to give Valerie an inquisitive glance.

"Nesting."

"Uh, I'm not a bird, Val. I'm not building a nest."

"I read in Redbook that women who are pregnant go through different phases in their pregnancy and one of them is called nesting. It's where they prepare their home for the arrival of the child. It's a real thing. You should read more, Rachel. Know what to expect when you're expecting and all that stuff. I see your boobs are starting to get bigger. That is also a sign that our baby is almost here. She's going to be one pampered baby. Start her young, I say."

"How much of that coffee have you had?" Rachel wrapped the paint roller in plastic wrap to keep it from drying out and climbed down the ladder. She was careful to find her footing, because her belly was so big, she couldn't see past the bulge.

"This is my second coffee. Gary and I always have some together before work if he doesn't get called out in a hurry. Anyway, I came to bring you the paper. They tried that Rider guy, aka John Smith, with the murder of Dolores and Angela, and attempted murder for trying to kill you. Guilty on all counts. He will never get out. Michelle's foster brother will also be in jail for conspiracy to commit murder, even though he allegedly didn't condone that or tell Rider to do it. Because he has priors though, he got another ten years. I feel sad for Michelle. Gary said that Rider was just looking for the right opportunity to be some serial killer. His profile basically said that he was nuts. And Michelle's brother just happened to pick the wrong guy, so he was right there with Rider. Messed up stuff."

Rachel took a sip of her tea. "I'm sure Michelle is upset, but we can talk to her more tomorrow night when she and Taz join us for dinner. I can't believe it's been over a year since all of that happened. I mean, I will always have the scars and I still have nightmares about seeing Angela like that, but time is helping. What I would not give to have Dolores here to see the baby when she comes. It was smart of you to hook Taz up with Michelle. I think they're cute together. It's not even weird anymore when we hang out together. Maybe it's because of knowing she's been through a shitty life and has never had female friends before. Lucky her that she picked us." Rachel raised her cup to Valerie for a toast.

"Yeah, here's to all of us." Valerie connected their cups. "Cheers!"

Rachel started waddling to the stairs and Valerie followed. They sat in the kitchen for more gossip time. Valerie ate a freshly baked cookie from the plate that Rachel placed between them. "Shirl said to tell you 'of course Rachel would have a baby that was late. Rachel herself is late for everything'. She cackled over that one. She said to tell you she misses you, but she is glad that you have a man that supports you staying home to raise your child."

"That was nice of her."

"Yeah, she is a good boss. Anyway, what's the verdict on baby names? What are we calling my niece? Given anymore thought to my list?"

"Your list made Gordon cringe. He is not going to name our child anything on that list. No Cheyenne, Asia or Dakota. We decided to name her after two very important women. Her name is Annie."

"You are naming her after me? I always thought my middle name was plain and boring. Anne doesn't incite excitement. Who else is Anne?"

"My mother's name is Margaret Ann. No E." Rachel reached for a cookie as she felt a warm and wet liquid run from between her thighs. "Oh God, Val. Call Gordon. Annie is coming."

"Okay! Do not panic! We got this. I'll drive you to the hospital and he can meet us there." She grabbed her phone and dialed.

Rachel placed her hand on her belly and gently rubbed to soothe her soon to be delivered child. "I have a bag packed. It's in the hallway next to the door! Let me clean myself up first. The doctor said first babies could take forever to be born, so I'm pretty sure we have time. Call my parents, too," Rachel said as she made her way back upstairs to the bedroom to grab some clean clothes.

The waiting room was filled with all the players. Valerie and Gary were planning the vacation they would take in the winter to get away from the cold. Michelle and Taz were talking about where they wanted to go for dinner since it did not seem like Annie was in any hurry to enter the world.

And the pacing daddy, Gordon, would give them updates each time a nurse came in to check on Rachel. She was never alone since her parents refused to leave. Gordon joined the gang in the waiting room and they noticed that he looked exhausted. "They said that she is almost fully dilated and it shouldn't be too much longer. Her mom is rubbing her head and her father is pacing. Between the two of us, we're wearing a path in the floor. Rachel is fussing over the half-painted bedroom. She wanted it done before Annie got here."

Gary handed Gordon a Coke and he took a large gulp. "Thanks," Gordon said, handing it back.

"Keep it, Gordy. You're gonna need the caffeine. Don't worry about the room. As soon as Annie gets here, the four of us are going to leave and get it done."

Gordon never thought that Michelle and he would ever be able to call themselves friends, but Rachel saw something in her that she liked. Her story of growing up without a real family made Rachel want to give her a chance. Taz was good for Michelle. He couldn't help but chuckle to himself that Taz wore a uniform. Sure it was scrubs, but still, some things never changed.

Mitchell appeared in the hall looking excited. "You better get in here, son. Annie is on her way. Mom and I are going to leave the room, but Rachel is calling for you.

Gordon hurried into the room to be there for his beautiful wife.

Two days later, Gordon and Rachel pulled up to their home. All the familiar cars were in the driveway. Valerie was unloading groceries from Gary's car, but stopped as she saw them pull up. "They're here!" she yelled.

Gary, Michelle and Taz came out of the house to help as they grabbed the things from Gordon's car. Valerie gave the bag she was carrying to Gary and claimed Annie. "My sweet little baby niece. Come to Auntie Val," she crooned and smiled as she held Annie close and carefully took her into the house.

Margaret and Mitchell were waiting with a bottle of champagne to toast to their amazing granddaughter. They were both excited to be able to visit often, since Rachel's new home was less than a mile away from their home. Mitchell slipped an arm around his daughter and pulled her in for a hug. Their relationship flourished and Rachel could not be more excited.

Margaret took a glass of champagne from Gordon. "To my beautiful Annie and daughter. Thank you to all of you. We are blessed to have you in our lives and look forward to many years with you in it."

Rachel drank a sip of champagne and was engulfed into Gordon's arms.

She hugged him back. "See what happens when you handcuff me to you in bed?" she whispered. "You end up with a wife and a child."

Rachel wanted more children. He would do everything he could to give her that dream. Gordon hugged her tighter. "I would handcuff you a million times over if it meant spending a million life times with you."

EPILOGUE

Valerie found herself pregnant shortly after Annie was born. She named her son Angelo to honor the memory of the fanatical Angela, a girl she would always remember as the person who managed to get her best friend as a roomy.

In the aftermath, Michelle and her friends were instrumental in getting an appeal for Eric. Since he hadn't actually conspired to murder anyone, and the conspiracy to get the notebook he had with Mayor Harrison did not actually break any laws, his sentence was reversed and he was released after spending ten months in county.

Mayor Harrison was exposed by Michelle as having an illegitimate daughter that he never acknowledged. The book was gone. The only proof she had that she was his daughter was a DNA test. Since he was not directly responsible for the murders of Dolores and Angela, he could not be charged with those crimes. But the public exposure hurt him badly and his run for the Senate proved to be fruitless. When it came time for re-election, he could not win the mayoral seat against what the public saw as a very strong and honest opponent—his daughter Michelle.

www.ingramcontent.com/pod-product-compliance
Lightning Source LLC
Chambersburg PA
CBHW071819190726
48292CB00005B/1515